Love

Is Never

Past Tense ...

A Novel

Janna Yeshanova

Love Is Never Past Tense ...

For information, please contact:
Life-Spark, LLC
3136 Kingsdale Center # 110
Upper Arlington, OH 43221
www.life-spark.com

To My Mom
&
My Daughter

Acknowledgments

I would like to express my sincere appreciation to Sergey Yeshanov, who coauthored the Russian edition.

I am extending my greatest thanks to my dear friend Jay Elkes, who was constantly by my side providing unwavering support. Without this person, the world of many people would be bleak.

My never ending thankfulness to my friend Seldar Atamov, whose priceless support was and is so significant for me and many others.

My sincere thanks to Kimm Nordman, who helped me with the Russian/English translation. We shared much laughter, tears and encouragement during our editing and birthing of this book. She gave her time and energy through many long days and nights to ensure I kept true to my story.

Melanie Martin-Jones, who not only helped me register the copyright in the book, but also informally advised me of many facets of publishing. Unable to put down the unedited first draft, she gave invaluable inspiration. *Thank you, Melanie.*

I offer my eternal gratitude to my friend, Becky Jarvis, who made a huge input in the final polish of the text.

I have to say *Thank you, Lina, for your support, advice and friendship* to my lifelong friend Lina Braykowskaya, who now lives in Israel.

Many thanks to my friend from Simferopol, Ukraine Dr. Yuri Kulish, who found for me the picture with this boundless sky for the cover of the first edition compensating the photographer with two bottles of vodka.

And I am so lucky to be able to find an outstanding graphic designer for the second edition cover, David Tonkin from Australia. *I offer my gratitude for your being so comprehensive in collecting and expressing the epic scope of the novel. Thank you, David!*

One more person! John Ondo with Ondo Media! My thanks to you, John, for the YouTube book trailer that everybody likes so much!

I am sure the word "thanks" doesn't have the capacity to appreciate all my friends all over the world for standing by me now, before and, I hope, after.

Thanks for opening my book.

Janna Yeshanova, 2013

Part 1

How It All Began

Part One: How It All Began

The old man sat on the stern of the boat, lowering his thin, wiry legs into the water. They were approaching the end of their days faster than their owner: the veins that had survived the surgeries had become a bluish, knotted spider web. The old man's feet were always cold, even during warm weather. But now the seawater, warmed by the sun, stroked them, pleasing him.

He had already been sitting like this for fifteen minutes, slowly moving the soles of his feet, every now and then dangling them over the water and then lowering them into the waves nearly lapping over the edge of the boat. It was quiet. The sun was shining high above the old man's head, casting its heat on his shoulders and the nape of his neck. It was time to turn the boat around, but he knew that soon enough the slow waves would eliminate the need, directing his vessel so that his back would face the sun. He could have sat at the bow of the boat, but then his feet wouldn't have reached the water. Besides, sitting like that wouldn't have been comfortable at all. What exactly is the point of these needless actions anyway, when time inexorably draws him to an event, the sole purpose of which he had sailed here? It was supposed to happen at sunset; when the sun dips down to meet the sea's horizon. This is what he had decided.

But now the sun was reaching its zenith, leaving him with an overabundance of time. He sat calmly, relishing his solitude ...

***

Long ago, there was a similar boat. A young and virile man rowed confidently, deliberately moving his female satellite away from the beach and the shrill sounds of a multitude of tourists. She reclined on the boat's stern, her long legs stretched out and her hands clasped behind her head. In this position her breasts achieved monstrous proportions. Once in a while, she bent towards the stern of the boat and lowered her palm into the water, enjoying how it streamed through her fingers. Of course, sitting on the narrow bench was not very comfortable, and she was constantly shifting positions, as if to tease him. Her breasts seemed to squeeze out of her swimsuit, evidently lacking a proper-sized container. Now and then she would adjust her top, tugging it up a bit higher, but sometimes she would forget, and the tips of her brown nipples would peek out, sending him into a frenzy. He strained at the oars, trying to exhaust his sexual energy; but, alas, his efforts were futile. As soon as they had moved far enough away from the shore, of course, he intended to move closer to her, and just let whatever was to happen, happen ...

Yet she sat calmly, completely oblivious to the rower—to her, it was a pleasant ride, nothing more. Sensing this, the oarsman wondered whether they would actually return to the shore in such an inglorious fashion. He had to surprise her, or at least interest her, for heaven's sake. But not a single word came to mind. On a schoolboy's impulse (that's essentially what he was, anyway), he suddenly got up and dove overboard. He wasn't a bad swimmer and was an even better diver, able to hold his breath for a long time underwater. Even now, he effortlessly reached the bottom. It was not deep—just five or six meters. Once at the bottom, he clung to a rock and waited as long as his lungs would allow. He and his buddies from diving class had always competed to see who could stay submerged the longest. He'd won every time, usually holding out for more than three minutes ...

At last, he could feel his chest tightening—he knew this was the signal to return to the surface. If you wait too long, you might not resurface, since you can momentarily lose consciousness. That's what their diving coach taught them. No one, of course, tried to prove him wrong. He released the rock and wound his way back to the boat, now a dark silhouette hanging picturesquely in the silver sky of the water—so seems the sea surface looking up from its depths. Purposely, he carefully emerged from the water at the nose of the boat, keeping himself hidden. Occasionally, he stole a glance at his companion, whose own gaze was fixed on the dark green waters. It was evident: worry was overtaking her. Having achieved his goal, he dove back down and immediately resurfaced right in front of her face, his wide smile expressing satisfaction. But instead of petting his long, disheveled hair, she again reclined, reminding him that it was time to return the boat to the shore; the time for their boat's rental was coming to a close. He scurried back on board and slowly started moving the oars, but the water seemed to thicken as if feeling his desire not to return to the shore.

***

During their first three days together, Serge (as they called our hero at the time) was the quieter of the two, once in a while muttering some insignificant phrases. The first time he saw her, he silently followed her for a long time. She walked along easily, shifting her long, rather well-proportioned legs. Her thin leather skirt swung from side to side, barely hiding her shapely hips. A green blouse tightly covered her beautifully straight back. All the while, Serge followed her like she was a vision, lacking the courage to come closer or to back away. He knew that making her acquaintance was a long shot; she was simply out of his league. How could he possibly know that she, a complete stranger, would inexplicably impact his life and be with him forever, whether she was at his side or not?

***

The awkwardly over-sized and battered ship wheezed as it fought its way through the waves. Inside the ship, something screeched and grumbled as if it were suffering from indigestion, but its motor blades diligently ground away at the water, leaving a long foamy trail in their wake. It had serviced workers daily over the years, providing transport to Oil Rocks, a legendary man-made island. Groups of student interns, Serge among them, would stare into the line of the horizon, hoping to be the first to witness this *world wonder*. Eventually, someone would exclaim, "I see it!" Everyone focused their eyes on the line between the sea and the sky, where they could see a barely noticeable dot. Soon the dot multiplied into many. They were spread out over the sea and, as one came closer, the contours of oil towers became apparent. The view was breathtaking, and became even more so when the scaffolding joining the oil towers together became clear. Half of the sea seemed woven together by a metallic spider web—in such a romantic place, destiny directed our heroes.

Half an hour later, the ship slumped to the pier with difficulty. The student interns grabbed their suitcases and quickly exited down the ramp onto the dock. Hardened oil workers, who made this voyage daily for work, followed them down the ramp onto the island. They swapped jokes as they passed by with those who were waiting to board. The appearance of these dark-skinned men, bodies permeated with petroleum, speaking an incomprehensible Azerbaijani language, combined with the gusty but warm wind and the hot sun hanging in the clear sky, created a colorful panorama, and expectations of spectacular adventures on this island tossed so far from the sea's shore. What was there not to like? The long waves of the Caspian Sea rolled beneath the dock; the green palisades were planted in wide vats with soil; and the tea-house, whose outer walls were overrun by grape vines, housed patrons sipping fragrant amber tea from tube-like glasses. It seemed like a resort, not an oil drilling site. Even when twelve people were forced to share a two-storied room in an old cabin, their enthusiasm remained; forty-five days of the Papuan lifestyle still stood before them.

After a week the men, like Robinson Crusoe, had already acclimated. Their faces became tan from the sun. Their muscles were firmer, thanks to hauling steel bars, sledge-hammering, and sawing boards. At first, it was terrifying to maneuver along the narrow beams hanging over the raging sea below, but later they became so accustomed to it they could do so like acrobats. They arranged a field around the oil scaffolding; this work was a result of the most serious technical expertise of its future engineers—water-based construction developers.

It seemed that after one month of staying on the island, they were fated to remain there for eternity. Everything was learned and then perfected. The scaffolding measured about two hundred kilometers in length. Of course, it made no sense to explore all two hundred kilometers, since if you'd seen one, you'd seen them all. They had had it with drinking tea and playing backgammon or dominoes, and the boys began to pursue the island's rarest commodity: the females, who spent days on end sitting behind desks doing office work. But in the evenings, the women would go to their own Lobnoye Mesto.[1] Sometimes movies would be brought to the island, and the benches of the outdoor cinema would be chock full of workers and interns. Twice they showed *The Dawns Here Are Quiet*. During the second showing, everybody vanished after the scene where the girls bathe in the nude.

Serge managed to find himself a rather simple-minded, thick-boned girl, but only because her species was endangered on this island: when there are no fish, even a crayfish is a fish. After two strolls with the girl, when there was nothing more to say, she pressed her plump body to Serge and began to wet her lips in readiness for a kiss. Serge obliged her lips a few times, and then promptly lost all interest. When he didn't like a girl or when he stopped liking her, he couldn't do anything about it. She became a "nobody" and a "nothing" to him.

It wouldn't be fair to call the girl disgusting. Her face wasn't ugly. But her short legs, the absence of even a hint of a waist, and her flabby breasts spoke for themselves. Serge became condescending and even cruel to her. But no, he didn't become vulgar or tease her—he simply ignored her, like she did not even exist. Perhaps this is the most horrible thing for any person, especially for a good-hearted, artless girl. She doggedly pursued Serge, but he became a master of elusion. But eventually, by some force of nature, their paths crossed at a party.

---

1 Lobnoye Mesto—Place of Skulls, a famous site in Moscow, Russia at the Red Square where public executions were held during the reign of Ivan the Terrible.

The boys had managed to get vodka (Oil Rocks was "dry", but if you paid six rubles, you could get all the vodka you wanted without problems). They found an old, abandoned well-hole where they hung out, and in a short time polished off two bottles. Having chatted for a while, the boys mingled with their girls, and the couples dispersed through the darkness in various directions. But Serge was left alone with his butter ball. The alcohol fumes made him excited, and so they climbed into the back of an old truck, which had stood without a hood and wheels since 1949, the year work began on Oil Rocks. Without prelude, he began to undress her. Her first breast flopped out, then her second. She helped him take off her dress and panties. It was stuffy and humid. There, in the middle of the sea, nothing was ever dry. Her wet body stuck to him like plaster, almost causing him to vomit. He told her that he was dizzy from bad vodka. He crawled off the truck and slowly staggered his way back home. His sole desire was to get into his bed; he didn't feel anything else. She quickly put her clothes back on and followed behind him, but this time did not try to catch up to him.

***

Serge didn't try to catch up to the shuffling, thin, leather skirt. He hadn't a clue what he would do if he actually caught up with her. So he continued following her along the high embankment for a fairly long time, until they crossed the whole of Lanzheron Park. But, reaching the beach, the girl quickly descended to the sea. Serge even began to jog a bit to keep her in sight. His head was clear this morning, and soon he would try out his cunning for the first but not the last time this day. The spy set up camp at the upper solarium and watched over her. Maybe she was waiting for some company, or a young man, or a girlfriend (which would undoubtedly seem to be better), but to our spy, all were equally bad possibilities. This guessing game carried on in his head, but it seemed she wasn't looking for anyone. She ducked into the changing room, and her leather skirt momentarily hung over the edge of the stall. After a minute, she exited, and Serge, pulling his long hair away from his head with both hands in anguish, groaned something unintelligible. Her breasts exited the little room first. The spot from where Serge looked down provided such visibility that his knees began to tremble. Her face was impossible to discern through her long hair and sunglasses, but something told him it would also be in order. She laid before her a light beach towel, and laying down she took a book from her bag and began to read. Burning her "landing site" into his mind, Serge took off like a shot to the nearest cabana rental. Fast as lightning, he exchanged his clothes for a key, crammed two metal rubles in the pocket of his swimming trunks, and became Don Juan. He feared, though, that there were already a bunch of admirers slinking ever closer to the sacred beach towel, and that he would simply be too late. He'd have to crawl to his place in line, and like the others, would have a poor chance of success.

He flew down the stairs and quickly found the beach towel, but ... its owner was nowhere to be found. There was a book, a beach bag, and sunglasses, but their owner had disappeared. Oh, yes! This would be the second time that a smart thought visited Serge's head today. People come to the sea to swim, after all! This interpretation of her disappearance comforted and delighted Serge. He became bolder and impudently tossed his glasses onto the same towel and cheerfully marched to the water. With his half-blind eyes he surely could not see her. And where, among dozens of bathers? He dove into a wave, and swam away from the shore. First, he couldn't stand to watch bathers jumping around like frogs in the shallow water. Second, at this moment, his exceptionally quick-witted head told him he couldn't be the first to return to her beach towel. Then he'd have to take his glasses and fiddle around a bit in front of the beach towel to buy time as he came up with a new plan. Perhaps he'd cover himself with the towel, or maybe ... no, he needed to work on his initial scenario.

He even came up with a sophisticated opening: "Excuse me, young lady, but I left my glasses here on your towel. I simply didn't have anywhere to put them, or myself for that matter." With this, his stockpile of ideas was depleted ...

At last he climbed out of the water and headed along the well-trodden route to her beach towel. The towel was in place, and on this towel lay the magnificent body of its hostess, but Serge's glasses were lying a little bit farther on the edge of the towel. Serge squatted down and mumbled his introduction. He was counting on her to respond with typical beach chit-chat: "Where are you from? How long ago did you arrive in Odessa?" or other such nonsense.

"Your glasses are fine," she responded. "I figured someone just confused their beach towel with mine, but have a seat anyway."

She scooted over, freeing up half the beach towel. He got scared. If he lay down, then he wouldn't be able to resist the urge to nuzzle up to her. Then he'd certainly look like a pervert, a youth brought up with no manners, or a pest—in a word, he would give the exact opposite impression than he wanted. He mumbled something like a "thank you" and lay down beside her on the sand. She motioned towards him with a little bag of sunflower seeds, "Help yourself."

"Oh God, what's this?" resounded in Serge's mind. "Are you kidding me ... sunflower seeds?" And his hand with a subsequent "thank you" reached in the bag.

"Do you like Ilf and Petrov?"[2]

"Lord, who is she talking about? I've only heard of them in passing, but I don't know the slightest thing about them..." Serge thought to himself.

"My name's Janna," she came to his rescue.

"Sergey," he stammered in reply, "but at the institute everyone actually calls me Serge, or Seriy ..."[3]

She chuckled.

"Grey. You're actually black as tar. Where did you get such a tan?" she asked, spitting out sunflower seed shells. Not even awaiting a response, she exclaimed: "Here is an interesting moment"—and she began to read her book aloud, something about Ptiburdukov and his Varvara, who was leaving her first husband for him but couldn't make up her mind. Janna read for a while, probably about five pages, and then thrust the book towards Serge and said, "You read from here," marking the place with her fingernail. Serge began to read, but he didn't understand a word. He was too busy worrying about his diction, trying not to miss any letters or words. He fought through two pages, but his audience was clearly not impressed.

"Would you like a cigarette?"

"If he has a smoke, then he'll stop reading." Serge could almost hear her thinking. He pulled a cigarette from a mashed-up pack of *Javas*, the best tobacco the Soviet Union could offer at that time. She handed him the matches. He brought the flame close to her face. She took a drag and rolled over on her back. Serge absolutely didn't

---

2 Ilf and Petrov—well-known Russian authors.
3 Seriy means "grey" in Russian.

know what to do: read, blow sand from her, ask her about something. But she was not waiting for any questions and didn't ask any questions. It was as if he simply was present. And that was that. The only thing that remained was for Serge to stare dumbfounded into the sand and observe the ants. Having smoked half the cigarette, she jammed the other half into the sand and turned back over on her stomach, brushing her leg up against Serge's. But she did not hasten to remove it. Silent Serge, who really didn't look the part of a reasonable person, turned into an animal. His uncontrollable desire sprang to life, pulling his swimming trunks down into the sand with such force that it became painful. Serge secretly burrowed a hole in the sand, easing the pressure. He became obsessed with a craving to climb on top of her. But this was out of the question, which made his desire even stronger...

"It's hot. Let's go for a swim," she said, lifting herself up on her elbows. For the first time he could see her breasts up close, causing his heart to leap through his ribs like a bird in a cage. He muttered he'd catch up to her, and when she left, his *desire* ever so slowly began to hide itself away, until he was finally able to get up and head towards the sea.

She splashed around in the waves, which towards midday became quite sizable. He flopped about next to her, often brushing up against her body. Then he suggested tossing her in the waves. He cradled her head and shoulders, gathered her hands into his, and finally lifted her up and tossed her into the waves. Janna liked it, and so did he, but for a different reason: every time she hit the waves, her bathing suit slid down slightly, and when her breasts finally became exposed, he was ready to splash to his very death. Suddenly, she ended up cradled in his arms. With one arm, she grasped his neck, and he now understood that everything will happen, he just needed to patiently wait.

Once something starts, eventually, it ends. The delightful swim as well: they returned from the water and again lay down on the beach towel.

"I want to get tanned like you." (She had already switched to the informal *you*[4] in the water. He liked this, as it made him feel less uneasy around her). She placed her arm next to his for comparison, and her brown skin seemed much paler than his almost blackened arm. Guiltily, he informed her that he just returned yesterday from his apprenticeship in Baku, and so it was not surprising that he was so dark.

"You have beautiful hands," she pensively remarked. Then, determined, she added, "No, you just wait. I'll catch up with you in two days. Just wait and see." These words poured over his body like oil. For Serge, this meant that he would spend at least two more days with her.

"Get some ice cream. Do you need some money?"

"I have it," answered Serge, but before he could get up and leave, he had to turn and crawl to hide his "desire"...

***

... It was becoming sweltering. The old man slowly got his legs into the boat and sprawled out on the stern, just as his companion had done so long ago. But the sun's rays were presented with a wrinkly chest, thick with grey hairs. Sweat began to accumulate in the folds of his skin. The old man grabbed a bottle of water and took a sip. Then he splashed himself with saltwater. He felt refreshed and more comfortable. He felt below his bench for the second

---

4 Russian has two forms of *you*: one (Vi) used in formal settings and one(ti) used with close friends and family members.

bottle, which he had in reserve for later when the sun would begin its evening descent. Peaceably, he closed his eyes and wound back the clock to decades ago.

***

In that distant '76, Serge found himself lying in a hospital bed for the first time, his leg raised and wrapped in bandages. His memory of meeting that enchanting girl, who was unlike any he'd ever seen, was as sharp as ever, dragging him back to '73 and Odessa. He had already had one varicose vein removed from his leg, which was now probably buried beneath some landfill. He felt sad. It seemed his future had shrunk to the size of a little window. He only wanted to return to the warm sea, take her in his arms again, cut through the foamy waves, and take full advantage of the opportunity purely to be with her ...

Around him, lying in partitioned-off beds, his fellow patients would usually fall asleep after lunch. After dinner, they fell asleep almost immediately. Many were given tranquilizers. In these hours, Serge would take to his notebook, and not paying too much attention to the beauty of the artistic word, would write, or more accurately record, a diary of those events of three years ago.

The old man remembered the contents of that diary almost verbatim, because he reread it over and over when he simply wanted to be with her, trying to understand why things turned out the way they did, and especially when life in a strange twist of fate drew them closer together ...

***

The sun was shining with the full force of its rays. The beach resembled a bee hive. The warm, murky sea was lapping its waters against the shore. The heat and humidity weighed down upon them. Serge lay flat on the towel. He slowly squeezed the sand in his hands and let it trickle in streams through his fist. She lay next to him, her gaze penetrating through the crowd of people into a place far off in the distance. Now and then, she would bring her cigarette to her lips and release a stream of smoke. Her hip pressed against his leg, and the spot of contact became moist. He sensed her body and wanted the moment to last for eternity. From the side, he could only see her profile. Barely turning his head, he could make out her beautiful nose, her full, extended lips, and her hair, which barely had a style and obviously knew nothing except a comb as it hung in charming disarray around her face. Round sunglasses hid her eyes.

Her long body tranquilly reposed on the towel, as if there was no heat, no people, not even him. At some point, he thought he was wasting his time. She was just toying with him. Next, she would say, "Bye, bye. Thanks for relieving me of my solitude." Or perhaps something even more ridiculous. She would take her things and leave, saying she had to meet up with her friends, or that she was getting a headache, or that she had PMS ... Shouldn't he stay one step ahead of her and get up and leave? What was actually holding him here? Absolutely nothing. In fact, all he needed was a little vacation fling. This was what he needed, having been imprisoned on Oil Rocks in the constant company of guys and the Azerbaijanis, who barely spoke a lick of Russian. The only thing that gave him consolation was their general good nature and their ability to laugh at just about anything.

But it was time for him to get away from everything. He'd had enough of those guys. Just over twenty days were left until the beginning of the academic year. So, why waste time? Gosh, around were multitudes of charming and simple-minded girls swarming about like small fish pecking at the guys. He, for all intents and purposes, was not exactly a monster. In his pocket he had a bunch of ten-ruble bills, earned by his sledgehammer on Oil Rocks. He'd wander along the beach, take a seat somewhere, or strike up a conversation, and perhaps ask a girl out for a night of dancing—and he could finally put an end to wracking his brains all the time about what to do or say. But this one lying next to him, torturing him, was not such a simple creature. She was like a cat—independent. She couldn't care less about the little boy fidgeting next to her. Seemingly accessible while in the sea, here she would keep her distance and then disappear in whatever fashion she deemed appropriate. What business should she have with a schoolboy who was oozing sexual desire?

Her hip was burning him. Some invisible little spiders quickly entwined them in a closely woven web. Young women, laying down or walking around, suddenly grew distant, and became minute and uninteresting. Next to him, there remained only her body—hot and powerful. There must have been a magnet setting at her core. It was buried deep, but revealed itself to Serge in a miraculous way ... Serge knew he was not going anywhere.

Then he rented a boat, and he skillfully navigated to the shore. She stood in the water up to her knees. She was holding her velvet flats and beach bag in her hands. Bathers entering and exiting the water turned to look at her. She just couldn't help drawing attention to herself. Her bathing suit was very daring, and her breasts clearly laughed at her vain attempt to cover them. It seemed that in due time the pitiful fabric wouldn't be able to hold out and would burst into shreds, yet it held on with its very last threads.

The girl, not even considering the possibility of her straps giving out, effortlessly situated herself on the stern as Serge took up the oars ...

When time was up, they returned and left the emptying beach behind them. On the way Serge took his things from the changing room lockers, pulled on his jeans and tee shirt, and smacked his bare feet along the hot asphalt, chasing Janna down. "Hmm, Janna! What a strange name. Not Tanya, or Olga—Oh, well ..." At sea he didn't even bother to move closer to her, or to touch her. Yet, oh, how he so badly wanted to climb down to the stern, tear off that damn bikini top, and well ... just the two of them in the boat and nobody around. The moment was lost.

"Wow, I could devour anything that does not move!" she literally and lucidly expressed herself. "Let's go chew on something."

On the terrace, where some wobbly chairs and tables stood, almost no visitors were sitting. They looked over the menu, but there was hardly anything there either, just a few dishes, thickly underlined with a dark blue pencil. Serge called over the waiter, who explained that the only thing left on the menu were *kupati*[5] and that they were running out of wine. However, acknowledging the shortage, the worldly waiter advised them to run down to a nearby store. Needless to say, bringing alcohol from outside to a restaurant was strictly against the rules, and if you didn't believe it, you could just look at all the empty bottles lying under the tables. Laws in the Soviet Union were made to be broken. When Serge returned from the store, Janna was tearing into a fatty piece of sausage in such frenzy that it looked like she had been starved for a couple of days.

---

5 *Kupati*—an Eastern dish made of sausage and includes a variety of vegetables.

"Sorry, I didn't wait for you. I just couldn't hold out any longer."

Serge poured the port into a couple of glasses, the sweet aroma gushing into their noses.

"Well, here's to our acquaintance ..." but his toast was quickly cut off.

"I can't stand banal phrases as 'to our acquaintance', or 'to meeting up'... ugh ... they just make me nauseous. Let's try without all that mess, all right, Serioga?[6]

"We could just get drunk and crawl over to those bushes without all these banal phrases."

"That's just plain vulgar! That's just as bad for my stomach as banality."

"Hell, it is impossible to approach you closer than a mile."

"Then don't try to please ..."

Serge grinned and polished off his wine. She too rather brazenly dried up her glass.

"Yuck, what garbage," she praised Serge's choice.

"Sorry, you buy what they sell."

"Fine then. If my cavalier doesn't offer anything better, he could at least give me a cigarette."

Serge opened up a pack of freshly bought *Opal* (a foreign brand, so they had to be good). She took a drag and began coughing. She recovered and suddenly began to laugh. Her laugh hardly resembled one of a lady, but it was very infectious. When she laughed, those around her could not help but join in. This was something already quite familiar to Serge, having witnessed this more than a few times.

"You know, ha-ha-ha, I've been thinking about our boat trip. If you had drowned, they probably would've put

---

6 Serioga—term of endearment for the name Sergey.

me behind bars. They'd say I struck you on the head with an oar ..."

"You surely would have squirmed your way out of it. You'd just tell them that I accosted you and badgered you with my stupidity, or even that I raped you. They'd surely believe you."

"Hey! What's with you?"

"What?"

"What's rape got to do with it? You were diving, sailor!"

"She tortures me now, becomes bold, when she isn't the least bit threatened," Serge thought to himself.

"Now I see ... maybe you're a eunuch? Hah-hah-hah!" as she threw back her head and laughed.

"All right, I'm taking off. I need to clean up and get a change of clothes. If you want, we can meet in an hour and a half ..."

She took her purse, ran up to the road, and in a minute she was sitting in a *Zhiguli,*[7] explaining something to the taxi driver.

***

In the evening, when nightfall had enveloped the city, the two found themselves on Chicherina Street next to a little half-subterranean restaurant.

Janna was dressed in a short, thin leather skirt and was wearing the same velvet flats as earlier. Suspended across her shoulder was the same little purse from the beach, matching her skirt. In her eyes (this time she wasn't wearing those sunglasses) shined a happy spark. She gave off an aura that said: "I've come to be entertained, let the festivities begin!"

---

7 Zhiguli—a Soviet-made Italian automobile.

Serge's appearance, however, hadn't changed. He languidly dragged himself home to his cousin's, with whom he was staying. To march almost to *Privoz*,[8] iron his pants and run at full speed across this sultry city? What for? She would think—that I want her to like me. "No, I don't. And the problem is not in the clothes. Was I walking after her outfit this morning?"

With all these thoughts, Serge hobbled to the agreed-upon spot, gorging on ice cream along the way. They sat on the tram, which rumbled along towards Arcadia, a well-known place for evening walks and a hangout spot for youthful escapades.

The alleys and paths were already teeming with partiers of every shape and color–beach life is always a holiday. Coming to such an atmosphere, Janna and Serge immediately became infected with the desire to "worthily" spend their time together. But what to do was not clear. They stood in a fairly short line to buy some smokes and two bottles of Crimean wine. Although this hadn't quite answered their question as to what to do, it calmed them slightly. In any case, Serge thought, "We'll find a nice spot to sit, drink some wine, and maybe lie down for a bit ... and so on ..."

As they went down an alleyway, Janna came up with a game: who could best imitate a passerby. The premise was that you had to walk up behind a pedestrian unawares and begin to parody his gait. The entire public was witness to this spectacle. People grinned as a vacationer turned around to see Janna in his face, unceremoniously drowning him in her drawn-out laughter.

One elderly woman, hunched over and helping herself along with her walking stick, shuffled along a roadway.

---

8 Privoz—Odessa's central market.

What a perfect target! Janna followed closely behind her all doubled up. Her movements were so precise, that Serge's ribs folded over with his laughter. The buxom, well-bred, young woman trailed behind the old woman, flashing her thighs now and then, groaning and murmuring something barely audible. One could discern the replica from the original only by looking at their ages. The old woman turned back and looked all around, but Janna shuffled along in her shoes. The old woman cheerfully swung her cane, aiming for the back of her prankster. But the prankster cleverly dodged the blow, hopped back a few feet, and flashed her bright teeth at the old woman.

Serge, like a young Pioneer[9], decided to support the initiative. Staggering up from the beach below was a man with his trousers hanging below his stomach. His head was covered by a handkerchief, tied at the corners in little knots. He'd clearly gotten sunburned and was drunk on beer or port wine. All the same, he seemed to be in good spirits. On his shoulder he carried a transistor radio, which rustily erupted with some invigorating melody. Serge began to beat out the rhythm and then, breaking in, came up directly under the guy's nose, inviting Janna with a gesture. They began to dance around the dumb-founded vacationer. But considering his condition, the man quickly understood what to do. He placed the transistor on the asphalt and began to spin on his not entirely vertical axis, every now and then clapping his hands over his head and then below his knees. He began to sing "Ochi Chernye"[10] ... while the speakers jingled the rhythm of a march. The onlookers began to gather. Serge got excited. Janna began lifting her legs high as if she were marching in a parade, at the same

---

9 Pioneer— the Soviet equivalent of "Boy Scout/Girl Scout", except being a Pioneer was a duty for most of the Soviet youth.
10 Russian: *Ochi Chernye*—Dark Eyes, a popular Russian folk-ballad.

time making faces and saluting to passersby. Serge grabbed the bottles by their necks and began beating them on his hips. But the march was cut off abruptly; a slow, rather melodic sound had taken its place, most likely something from Paul Mauriat.

Serge lowered the bottles next to the receiver and gallantly invited Janna for a dance. They embraced as close as was fashionable at that time: she grasped his neck, and he placed his hands on her waist, so low, that you could hardly call it a waist. A few other couples joined in on the improvised dance floor. Janna joyfully looked into Serge's eyes. Her lips melted away into a smile. Serge gently touched the very edge of her lips, drawing her closer to him. But the melody stopped. The news nobody needed started and the crowd which had just gathered started dispersing.

"Well folks, I am done playing with you," said the guy, watching the departing crowd, almost on the verge of tears. He bent down to pick up the transistor. He noticed the bottles. And he became frozen like a statue.

"Oh no, everything is fine guys!" He became more cheerful, and with an unsteady hand he picked up a bottle. "Is it for me? Like payment for a choreographer?!" he asked.

"You already drank your scales, buddy." Serge slapped the guy's palm. On the palm remained fifty kopecks. "That's for keeping us company."

The guy thrust the coin into his pants, saying: "This is good, *dzhenkuju.*"[11] Moving his face closer to Serge's, he breathed on him with fumes of alcohol.

"The girl you have is top notch! I feel it! Don't miss it!"

"All right, pops. Where are you from?"

---

11 Dzhenkuju— Polish: thanks.

Pops didn't hear a thing. All he could do was blankly stare into the distance as he started singing about his enemies burning down his little hut. Slowly, he began to wander back his own way.

***

... On the beach it was twilight and chilly. The wind, though warm, blew in violently from the sea. Serge and Janna settled themselves on a slope. Next to them was a large acacia bush, which provided them a cozy shelter despite the howling wind. The loud, gray sea surged below. It frothed and splashed along the concrete seawall and rocks. The waves hissed when receding back to the sea, fighting with their sisters who rushed headlong towards the coast. The picture was frightening, but bewitching. Serge could have sat like this for hours and watched the surf, that is, if he were able to tear his eyes away from Janna. The waves and Janna were aesthetic equals, and there was no need to spin his head from one to the other.

Serge placed the bottles on the limestone. He took one and pushed the cork inside. Janna took two sips and passed the bottle back. Suddenly, she became gloomy and pensive. Such mood swings in people always discouraged Serge. He never knew what to do in such cases. There wasn't even a visible reason for change.

"Want some more?" he asked.

"Nah," she replied sharply.

"And why not?"

"Don't ask."

"You want me to finish this all by myself?"

"At your discretion."

"Oh yea, then I'll be singing drunken songs, like ole' Pops, and hover over you."

"I'll run away."

"What for? You wouldn't want to miss it."

"Well drink. Maybe then you will start talking and will say something amusing ... You mute."

Serge put the bottle to his lips and sucked down about three-quarters of its contents. He wanted to drink it all out of anger, but it almost caused him to vomit. He put the bottle back on the ground and looked at her. She remained stone-faced. Serge got out his cigarettes, put them next to him, took one up, and lit it. When he put out the butt, Janna was shivering.

"What's the matter? You cold?"

"Nah, it's nothing."

"Are you reminiscing?"

"Mind your own business."

"Then drink. In wine is truth, they say."

She grabbed the almost empty bottle of wine and stared into it, deep in thought. Serge felt his body warm as the first alcoholic fumes weighted his brain. He looked at her drawn-in legs, the arms which clasped her knees, and her face with full lips. No matter how hard she tried to appear boyishly outgoing, it was clear to Serge that next to him sat a woman. Moreover, her womanhood manifested itself so intensely that his body, soaked in the fresh, aromatic wine, wanted so badly to caress and kiss her—just as badly as he longed for the stormy sea. The only thing he did not want to do, however, was to dig into her thoughts and try to understand what was inside of her. Forces of nature drew him to her. He didn't give a damn what she was thinking or what she would think later. How she lives, what are her interests, or who she is in general. Next to him sat a woman—young, attractive, and surely passionate. All passionate types have their sudden changes of mood. It's like the ebb and flow of the tide. If she were half as temperamental, she would still have plenty. But how could he turn this temperament to his favor? ...

Serge grabbed the second bottle, put it between his legs, and turning to Janna, said, "I wouldn't have ever imagined that you'd become like this. We came to have fun, to act up; but if you've had a change of heart we can just call it a night. What's the point of sitting in silence? It's as if we're dragging our feet ..." He stopped short. Her eyes stared into the distance, and her lips began to whisper:

"Odessa sleeps silent,
Breathless and warm,
The night is mute, and the moon adorns,
A curtain, light and transparent,
Enveloping the sky. No sound can be heard;
'Cept the Black Sea's surge ..."

And then she quietly added, "Oh, my precious boy, I know what you want."

"Of course you know. It cannot be hidden."

"But it won't happen!" she sternly retorted, without the slightest hint of a joke.

"Well, that makes it easier for us to go our separate ways then. And never, ever get together again! You torturer, sadist!"

Serge clearly understood that now the day was practically lost. Why should he bother anymore with this strange girl? Now he'd hear some stories about her past romantic mishaps and how she didn't want to repeat those mistakes. She may even tell him that she has a child (which doesn't look to be true at all) and that she couldn't be immediately intimate with a complete stranger. And all in all, he was not her type. But glancing at her, he saw tears. Their eyes met; two big drops trickled naturally down her cheeks. But suddenly she began to laugh loudly, and Serge began to feel goose bumps running along his spine. Then, through her laughter she grabbed the wine, focused on the bottle for a minute, and tossed it away.

"Open the next bottle," she commanded, rubbing her lips, reddened from the last bottle. Serge hurried to hand her the second bottle. She took several more sips, ate a chocolate candy, and began to smoke ...

Serge drank almost the entire bottle, leaving a bit in the bottom, and lay down on his back, attempting to understand something, but couldn't understand anything. She took the last hit of her cigarette, had a sip of wine, and started down the slope towards the asphalt.

They went along the riverbank, Janna again holding her silence. Both thought their own thoughts. Actually, Serge really wasn't thinking about anything. He had become a bit down. But the wine had done its job, he felt that emptiness in his head, and he decisively didn't want anything. Even her shapely, firm legs couldn't grab his attention.

On a stone guard rail sat an elderly woman selling boiled shrimp. Serge bought a bag and walked along eating them, spitting the shells to the side. If she had turned around and left, he would just deliberately walk his way. He cooled towards her. He became indifferent to her.

He turned on a breakwater where at the end, some fishermen sat covered with tarps to protect themselves from the sea spray, trying to catch smelts. She walked along beside him, but if she had decided to turn around at that very moment, Serge would have hardly followed her. In fact, now she was following him, and he liked it. It was dark on the pier, the wind tossed their hair, and the sea was spraying, smacking into the concrete flood wall. Gazing into the mutinous waves, they had no desire to become better acquainted with them.

"Are you up for a swim?" suddenly inquired Janna.

Serge handed her the shrimp and began to tug off his shirt. Janna waited, while he undressed, then grabbed him by his hand and said:

"Listen, let it go. I was just joking. I forgot that you are a bit drunk." And then laughingly added, "The sea seems shallow to you now."

"Where was your pity when I was undressing? What am I supposed to do, get dressed again? What am I, a puppet? If you want—you undress me. If you want—you dress me. And then, what does it mean that I am drunk? ..."

Serge, considering that he had a fairly firm and sober head on his shoulders, was insulted.

"I'll drown. Then you'll bite your elbows.[12] Or maybe you won't. Whatever you'd like."

And he dove into a rather tall wave. He had a devilish desire to just drown so that his body would be ejected onto the concrete. Janna would fly over; tear at her hair and wail, "Poor me. I brought a poor young boy to his death. Oh my boy, my precious, come back. I beg you! Ohhhh! I fell in love with you! Ohhhh! Someone give him a magic elixir..."

Serge drew up this scene in his mind, diving through the waves. But the desire to drown was gone. He floated out to open waters, and then returned ... but he couldn't see the shore. The next wave picked him up, and then the shore came into view. Serge imagined Janna rushing along the concrete shoulder, and he turned back to shore.

He crawled up onto the wet concrete, almost scraping his knee. Janna was sitting silently. Serge stood by her side, not embarrassed to take off his swimming trunks and wring them out. Then he put his pants back on his wet

---

12 To bite your elbows—Russian phrase meaning that it is impossible to bite your elbows, but something is so terrible that miraculously you are able to bite your elbows.

body. He wanted to move close to her, kiss her, and spit to the side in disdain like they do in the movies, but instead he picked up his bag of shrimp and started walking away.

Up above, in the shrubbery, was a stone gazebo. It seemed that nobody was there. Serge turned around. For a long time they stared unblinkingly into each other's eyes. Then he took her by her hand and pulled her along a steep trail. But climbing up like that wasn't comfortable for either of them, so they switched places, and Serge helped Janna up, supporting her by her hand and reveling in this presumptuousness. Soon they reached the stone terrace. The gazebo was constructed in the standard post-war style. Round columns supported the massive roof. The only thing lacking was an alabaster statue of some horn player or a girl with a bowl. Instead, there was a different, live girl. She sat in the depths of the gazebo, on a pile of straw from God knows where, and next to her sat a guy who looked like a gnome in the grass. Serge went up to the edge of the gazebo and stared down into the dark expanse, where below, almost invisibly, hissed the sea. A distant ship flickered its lights, pointing out where the water ended and where the sky began.

Janna approached Serge, resting her elbows on the fence, which was thick as a boa. In the dark, her shape seemed timid and even tender, although, he certainly hadn't noticed any tenderness coming from her the whole day. She abashedly looked at the ends of her fingers. She clenched them together as if she were asking for forgiveness for their unwarranted interruption of the sentimental couple below. Serge sensed a timid request to leave. But he knew he wouldn't leave. Now, he felt a power over those bodies hiding in the shadows. He felt a power over Janna, remembering how they reached the gazebo, how he touched her firm legs with his head, and how carefully and quickly she planted her feet on the sharp stones of the trail. She hadn't left or deserted him. Recalling this, he experienced a new sense of security. How the hell could they have known that this place was occupied? After all, there was no sign.

The straw rustled. Serge turned around, pulled a cigarette from his pocket, and asked for a light. Darkness responded—no matches.

"Well, I guess I'll have to use my own then," Serge replied like a high school sophomore. He took out his box of matches and struck one, lighting up the gazebo. On the straw sat two offspring of humanity: a man of about forty, with a large belly and the pitiful countenance of one of Chekhov's officials, and a woman of about the same age. She quickly shuffled her skirt up to her knees, moving farther off into the shadows. The match's flame exposed those guilty eyes, and it seemed the couple would get down on their knees and pray: "We are sinners, father. Sinners. May our souls repose ..." Janna sputtered with laughter. Serge made a supercilious grimace and lit his cigarette. He wanted to shout, "Get out of here you shameless...!" But turning to Janna, he took hold of her elbow, gently pulled her close to him, saying: "Let's leave them." They took a few steps before noticing two silhouettes slithering through the shadows, abandoning the solemn spot of straw.

"Well isn't that nice of them," Serge said, sitting down on the warm straw, leaning up against a column. Janna mirrored his actions.

"Give me a cigarette!" The word "please" was clearly not part of Janna's vocabulary.

Serge handed her the pack. While Janna tapped her cigarette, Serge watched the match burn his fingers; finally Janna lit it up:

"Well that was amusing, wasn't it?"

"Yep. We've been amusing others all day. Now it's their turn to amuse us."

"So you were watching how others were staring at us, getting a kick out of our antics? I was hoping that you were only staring at my legs!"

"I won't hide the fact that I was staring at them. I'm no worse than the others, who you were teasing all day. You were glowing so much I swear you could've blinded someone."

"You're not so bad yourself. But did you know that your jeans are torn a bit in the back?"

"And is it that noticeable?"

"Why, does it bother you?"

"Taking an example from you—not at all. Everyone's been getting pleasure out of your little black panties."

"Hah, well what if they did? At least mine are in one piece. Your butt is full of holes, you ragamuffin."

"Then why are you dealing with ragamuffins?"

"Oh dream on ..."

"You're just kissing up for another smoke, you little beggar."

"Yea ... like I really need to smoke your smelly cigarettes!" she retorted, tossing away another butt. Looking at him victoriously, she opened a caramel and placed it in her mouth. Her lips were right next to his, and he kissed them easily.

"Let me finish chewing it, you overzealous ..."

He squeezed her tighter. Her head swayed from side to side, and her full lips poured a blissful aura across his body. His hand crept up and grasped her breast. It was big and firm. "And she hasn't even had a child yet," Serge confirmed in his mind. But Janna commandingly moved his hand away. Then, he clasped her face, peppered her with kisses, swept her up off her feet, and placed her down upon the straw. He pressed her tightly in a fevered embrace. She threw back her head, exposing her neck for kisses. Serge grazed his nose into her shoulder, smelling the scent of freshly tanned skin still holding the sun's rays. His excitement grew quickly. He rolled on top of her, giving her the full brunt of his weight. Her breathing became irregular and short, but to Serge it seemed to burn, turning him into an animal. He didn't even attempt to undress her. That sweet moment had almost arrived, threatening to spill out all over the place, just seeking some release. Janna felt his hardness on her stomach, sobering her up, and so she began to tug at his jeans, attempting to slide out from under him.

"That's enough Serge," she whispered insistently.

One more minute and his volcano would have erupted. Then a faraway thought came to him, whispering, "Well, I will have to go to the sea to wash out my pants ..." He promptly rolled over to the side, breathing heavily and feeling his pulse pound through his body ... His volcano calmed itself; the eruption didn't happen. He lay for a few more minutes, now feeling his bladder might erupt instead. He excused himself and went off into the bushes. The evening lingered with freshness. Cold stars hung in the translucent sky, lighting his path. They also seemed fresh. Feeling relieved, Serge returned to the terrace, but Janna was nowhere to be found. He wanted to call out to her, but he could hear a steady stream literally steps away.

"What? Am I not a human being?" shouted Janna, laughing with her startling, vibrating laugh. She emerged from the bushes fixing her skirt, which was clinging to her panties from behind, and Serge collapsed onto the ground from laughter. She plopped down on his stomach.

"Why are you laughing?" she asked.

"Why wouldn't I laugh? Now it appears that urine is bringing us closer, but I was hoping that something else would."

"Wow! What haven't we done already! Ha-ha-ha!"

"Well, it may be enough for you to go pee into the bushes, but it's not enough for me." Serge raised himself, crawling up underneath the fringe of her skirt.

"That's to be continued, but not now," she said gleefully, pulling his hands away again.

"How old are you?" she asked unexpectedly.

"Why? Are you afraid to seduce a minor?"

"Well, I'm waiting."

"Twenty-one and a half," Serge lied, having only turned twenty a month ago. "And you?" he asked automatically, immediately realizing how impolite that was.

"You're not supposed to ask a lady that sort of question, but I'm older than you."

Serge figured the difference was about two or three years, maybe a bit more. Good lord, what a ripe woman! She wasn't a girl who had never been kissed. What would it cost her to snuggle up to a guy with a burning sexual desire? She can see that I am burning. She wants it, too, but is shying away. Light her a smoke, or don't even speak to her—she'd do anything to run away from her responsibilities. She's not a fool; she actually understands everything.

A slight chill came over her body.

"Are you cold?"

"A little bit."

Serge quietly took off his shirt and covered her shoulders. Her hands were folded around his waist.

"Are you freezing?"

"It's completely up to you, mademoiselle."

"At least put my tee shirt on."

"That wasn't exactly what I had in mind."

She tossed his shirt aside, crossed her arms, grabbed the sides of her shirt with her hands and pulled her tee shirt over her head. Serge was stunned—maybe it was happening. Her hair got caught in her collar, and she struggled to free it. Yet Serge couldn't take his eyes off of her body, its tan lines noticeable from underneath her bra. He held her gently and unfastened the hook. His heart pounded at his ribs like a sledgehammer. He wanted so badly to envelop her half-naked body but restrained himself, falling back down onto the straw. Now, the initiative was up to her. She could pounce on him like a panther. Oh, how badly he wanted that! Instead, she crawled deeply into his shirt and shriveled up. Serge wasn't very comfortable lying with his naked torso on the prickly straw. He got up, came up to her from behind, lifted her up and placed her feet on the ground. Holding her by her hand, he led her back down the pathway from the gazebo. They quickly descended to a well-lit alley and walked along towards the park's exit like longtime lovers. Serge threw her tee shirt on, and Janna, chuckling, poked at his bellybutton with her fingers. He took her up into his arms, carrying her a few steps, and then lowered her back to the ground, pressing his face to hers and kissing her gently. They walked through the park, exited onto the street, and trudged toward the city.

Well into the night, the two parted on the corner of an empty street. Janna cloaked herself in her shirt again. Serge tied his shirt around his waist in a knot. They said their goodbye for a while, now and then kissing and discussing the next day's plans.

Eventually, the distance between them increased as Serge turned the corner. It seemed to him that this girl excited him, and not only sexually ...

***

The next morning Serge arrived on time at the agreed-upon location: the corner of Deribasovskia and Soviet Army. He paced around, observing the scurrying pedestrians, finally making out Janna running towards him, slipping her way through the crowd. She was ten minutes late, so Serge, hiding behind the trunk of a tree, toyed with her. She flew by a few meters from him and crossed the street, stopping to look around. Serge left his hiding place, heading in her direction.

"Hey. Do you normally run in the mornings to break a sweat?"

"No, I needed to make it to the furniture store on time," she made up on the fly, although there weren't any furniture stores in the vicinity.

"So what, you are late. Is the store closed now?"

"I saw you. Why would I need furniture now?"

"What do you say I am—a night stand? A dresser? Maybe a bed. You know, I can be your bed."

"What would I do with such a *bed*? I would fall off or cut myself on your bones."

"Just put some pillows around me."

"Listen. Now that's an idea! You'll lay all covered in pillows, pretending to be my drunken prince."

"Why drunken?"

"Are you ever sober? Could've fooled mee-ee!"

"And what ... you'd be the princess?"

"Yep!"

"Also drunk."

"But of course I'd be drunk ... because of you. And I would ask you constantly, how can I serve you, what is your desire?"

"I think you probably know what I'd like."

"Yeah, but you're not a prince just yet, and you're not drunk either ..." said Janna, but Serge wasn't listening. Instead, he was kissing her chilly morning cheeks.

They hugged and set off towards the bus stop, which was located a bit lower on the opposite side of the street.

***

The city had awakened. Southern cities are early to rise. The day began and with it, a new life. The Odessans were already bustling in the streets as if they were preparing for an evacuation. They rushed along, nervously gathering at the city's public transport stop, storming the trams, trolleys, and buses. Housewives scurried about the stores and shops, searching for the best deals and the tastiest morsels. Visitors, on the contrary, behaved as if they'd decided to remain in the city forever. Draped in cameras with exposure meters, they strolled at their leisure, dallying at the souvenir stands. "Dark blues, dark blues, who wants dark blues?"[13] Onions, cucumbers, reds![14] Everything fresh—they were just growing! Hey lady, why did you turn away? Look at this beauty ... Dark blues, dark blues!"

"Why are you shouting at the whole street? What kind of dark blue are they—the ones you have are actually yellow," Janna shot back.

"Say what, are you color-blind? To color-blind people I do not sell. Depart and do not bother me ..."

Odessa woke up and entered a new day. The colorful public thronged the streets. Girls flitted in short dresses. Old women shuffled in long chintz, and men hid their heads in straw hats.

---

13 Dark blue—local reference to eggplants.
14 Reds—local reference to tomatoes.

Serge was hiding nothing. He had a reliable enough cap of tow-headed hair which was bleached out from long wandering in the southern latitudes.

A trolley bus arrived at the stop. Serge managed to be one of the first passengers and they sat down on the hot, fried leather seats. Serge delicately sat down next to a window and imagined himself as a cactus in a greenhouse. In a minute the palms of his hands became wet from sweat, and his shirt and trousers stuck to his body. The trolley bus was filling up and someone was constantly pushing Janna. She drew nearer to Serge, and he appeared to be squashed from both sides: the heated covering of the bus on one side—Janna's flaming hip on the other. Serge looked out of the window at the cypresses going past. Janna adjusted her skirt—not downwards, but upwards—which was a mistake. Almost two months and one more night of holding back had taken its toll on Serge. The desire to possess this woman, like a snake, crept into him. In his softened body only one muscle strained. It climbed into his pant leg and hid. Serge understood that it would pursue him all day long … yes, Odessa had definitely woken up!

They rolled on the beach while the sun, tired from work, began to go down to its evening quarters. Janna lay in the sun the whole day, promptly catching up to Serge's skin color. He swam far way, then flopped on the hot sand. Janna had brought along a copy of *Golden Calf*, but neither of them read it: it could only lay forlornly nearby, giving nary a moo. Because of the heat, conversation took too much effort. Serge only learned that Janna was a philologist, and she lived in Kishinev. She came to Odessa to rest for five days and to meet some friends. But her friends were nowhere to be seen, and Serge hoped that they not show up at all.

Janna's skin became red-bronze and they moved under a tree. Here it was cooler, and the important thing, it was far from people. She changed into a different swimsuit, a yellow one. She lay before him easy, shamelessly enough, and unperturbed. Probably she reveled in her authority over him. But only she could know this. No conversations about their relationship took place. Actually no conversations took place at all. Sometimes they exchanged meaningless phrases. But mostly they were silent.

Serge was constantly struggling with his hormones that seemed to live autonomously and manage his brain, and not vice-versa. Nothing was coming into his mind. Somewhere, Grandpa Freud was celebrating.

Above her upper lip, droplets of sweat had formed. He got up, and with the tip of his tongue cleaned them off. She did not stir at all. She did not draw him closer and she did not push him away. Serge clasped her lips and gently began to inhale them into himself, and to release them slowly.

"You kiss well, only your moustache is a little prickly," she whispered as she raised his head. "Let's go and drink something. Thirst tortures me."

They drank beer, warm and sour. A little man with a bristly face went around and sold dried up salty anchovies. From him dripped rotten ooze and yesterday's vodka, and nobody wanted to buy his fish. Out of pity, Serge bought a big paper scoop full, but they had to throw out almost all the fish as they were covered in solid salt.

They went along the park, sat on a bench, ate ice cream, kissed because of Serge's permanent desire, and talked a little bit about themselves. Serge said that he was an Odessan. More precisely he was born in Odessa, but, unfortunately, did not live in this city. He lived in Moscow, but more correctly, near Moscow. He had a sister. Two, really—one in Odessa, who was actually his cousin, and the other, his true sister, living in Moscow, who would soon arrive with his parents ...

"I only have my mom," Janna replied. "My dad passed when I was nine and a half. She is by herself now in Kishinev and I need to go to her soon." Her sad voice immediately became more cheerful. "But I have a lot of friends and acquaintances. Guys and girls. They are like brothers and sisters to me."

Near the exit to the park stood a scale, and behind it sat a lean, black as tar, old geezer who took two kopecks from interested people to measure their weight. Serge appeared to weigh 73 kilograms, and noted that he had lost 3 kilograms since the beginning of summer. Janna was a whole 10 kilograms lighter, but to Serge it seemed that she should weigh the same.

They had dinner in a small green cafe fenced in by a slanting lattice with ivy twisted around it. It was the custom to share tables at Russian restaurants, and a *middle-aged* couple was brought over to sit at their table. The man appeared reserved. The woman chattered about everything, but basically about herself. She was thirty-five years old and was still never married. And here, at last, she met the person to whom she will belong to from now on, and this person will belong to her too. The man vaguely assented, but was engaged more in a piece of tough meat, as if it was cut out of a heel. The woman became excited and started to foretell happiness for Serge and Janna. She envied their age, and told them about what unbelievable opportunities were coming for them, and poking her beloved in the side, kept on repeating, "Well, why aren't we at least twenty-five?"

Janna was rather bothered, and in a fairly loud voice, she directed Serge's attention to how the woman chomped noisily and made smacking sounds with her lips and how this provincial holds a fork and that she had no concept about the purpose of a table knife. Eventually, Janna began to scoff frankly at the ignorance of their neighbors, and the man thought that it was necessary to say goodbye and go home.

Janna and Serge laughed at them for a long time, copying and mocking them. "I'm already thirty-five, and I still haven't put out! And it would be so desirable to have children! Yes, swell me up with kids, but my man is only interested in gorging on meat ..."

"But maybe he is not capable?" Janna whispered conspiratorially, with her lips attached to Serge's ear. Serge did not miss a moment of even her slightest approach, and kissed her. "How did you guess, tell me secretly."

"You won't be able to understand. It is a complex combination of intuition, visual observation and hypnotic penetration into depths of a human being."

"Yes, it is more difficult than physics."

Suddenly, they saw some people in the street selling milk, and having refused dessert, they ran outside like children. The milk was fresh and tasty. Janna drank directly from the package and large white drops fell on her skirt. She wiped them, laughed, drank again, and the drops fell once again ...

The sun had tiredly fallen down behind the trees when the couple came across an amusement park with loud laughter. There were many adults and children, and everyone wished to receive their share of pleasure. Shouts and shots reached everywhere, and they heard sirens and howls from the attractions. Janna wanted to take a ride on a roller coaster. It went upwards, downwards, zoomed through a tunnel, turned sharply, and everyone squealed in delight. But there was a long line of people waiting for that delight. Janna went to the beginning of the line, chose a very tall guy, and asked if she could go in front of him. When he saw Serge approaching, his face turned to curdled milk, but he shrugged his shoulders and mounted the roller coaster by himself.

The ride was really not bad. The car sped up and rushed in a circle. When it moved down, something inside your stomach flipped and somehow was squeezed in a special way. It was pleasant. But soon, you get used to the sensation, and you don't catch your breath in excitement as much. To squeeze out more pleasure, Janna and Serge kissed, and they kept kissing until the car stopped. Leaving, Serge felt many pairs of eyes on him, as he held his head high with pride because of the tan-skinned, graceful girl with a high bust who went with him, and who he had embraced for so long ...

In half an hour, the taxi arrived at her house. She seldom went by public transport. The taxis were at her beck and call.

"My friend George lives here, but I'm staying at his house. Let's go. I will introduce you to him."

"Now the friends are showing up!" thought Serge with bitterness, and he said that he had no desire to get acquainted with anyone.

"You'll see—he is a dear person."

"I'm sure he is. But that doesn't obligate me to meet him. I will wait for you here."

She disappeared within a gate, and Serge sat down on a bench. With a worried face, he glanced around. A few minutes passed. Janna jumped back out in the street, grabbed his hand, and dragged him behind her.

"There is nobody there. I started feeling sorry for you. I won't change my clothes that fast."

Serge entered the darkened premises filled with old furniture. Here everything was in order, like in a crypt.

"George lives with his grandmother. He is twenty-eight years old. He is like my older brother ..." Her voice was coming out from the bathroom, where she was trying to build something on her head.

"All this is pleasant," Serge thought. "George, his grandmother ... I wonder where they find room for themselves. I would not say there is a lot of space. And this corner probably belongs to George." There stood a cheap tape recorder, and some scientific works lay upon the shelves. In the same place, there was an armchair-bed—one berth. The second was the ancient sofa but even though Serge did not try, he doubted he could thrust even a folding bed in here. George, he concluded, was probably some extreme ascetic. "I could not sleep in such close quarters with a woman and not become her lover. But maybe ... Oh yeah, but the grandmother ... oh look what I found to stuff my head with. Isn't it all the same to you? Soon this wonderful summer romance will end. Enjoy it in the meantime ..."

Serge sat on a chair and inhaled the crude dampness of the room. In the bathroom, some bottles rumbled, and Serge became bored.

"You keep me waiting, madam!" Serge rose and stood in the doorway of the bathroom. Janna stood in a bra and was angrily washing her face.

"You'll live! Get out of here."

Serge left. He took a book from the shelf and flipped the pages. It featured drawings of people's intestines, from different angles. With disgust, Serge put the book back in its place. Janna came from behind him and put her hands on his shoulders. He turned. Her face smelled of freshness and fragrant soap. It was hard for him to keep himself together ...

"Are you ready?" he asked, tearing himself off her lips with difficulty.

"Ooh, quite."

She put on shoes, put her handbag on her shoulder, and they left.

Outside, it was stuffy. The setting sun shone on the roofs of houses, and on the asphalt long shadows were crawling. Janna ran out in the street and immediately stopped a taxi, then climbed in the front seat. She never sat down in the back seat if a front seat was available. Having taken her seat, she turned to the driver and asked, "Is it OK to smoke here?" She never received a negative answer. She always knew where to go, where to get out, and what to talk about with the driver, and found out all kinds of interesting information from him. Serge looked at the nape of her neck and felt safe.

The driver appeared to be garrulous and with an amusing Odessan accent told them what sites to see, what cafe was the most popular, what was happening at the opera theatre—it seemed he knew all about the city and loved it very much. (Although, you will never meet an Odessan who does not love and is not proud of the city.)

The taxi stopped at Deribasovskia Street, at the big glass shop where jewels were sold. Serge rushed to jump out of the car to open the front door for Janna. She loved it when men took care of her, and considered it ground rules for good manners.

"Why do you give me *so much*, citizens? You won't have enough for ice cream," the taxi driver said sarcastically, recounting the money. With a feigned feeling of pity, the driver pretended to be on the verge of tears. "Oh, will it be enough? Then give me more, please, that I could also get some ice cream." In this way, he extracted twenty extra kopecks, and they did not mind at all giving him the extra. Everybody laughed, waved to each other, and the taxi driver got his next passengers.

Deribasovskia Street is the most animated spot in Odessa. Every tourist, knowing nothing about Odessa, will ask where to find Deribasovskia—the central street of this distinctive city. Every person in the USSR knows about this street, because if a person talks about Odessa they will necessarily mention Deribasovskia. Or they will talk about it in their next joke: "We asked an intelligent passer-by wearing glasses carrying a thick portfolio, 'How do you get to Deribasovskia?' He carefully put his portfolio on the pavement and pronounced, 'I wouldn't want to confuse you, but you are standing on it.'" Kotia, Monia, and Spirah, Serge's best friends from his Odessa childhood, often invited him to go watch the crazy tourist characters on Deribasovskia. Really, would the founder of Odessa, the Neapolitan Deribas, expect that he would become an eternal contemporary of the people working on the street named after him!

Here were all kinds of people, small ones and big ones. Nimble, swarthy children darted between the legs of adults; respectable old men sedately walked with their elbows intertwined. Cars continually approached the curb of the roadway. They left with elegantly dressed youth: girls in long dresses, wearing big round sunglasses in a silver frame, and young men in stylish Finnish[15] trousers and fitted multi-colored shirts.

Serge's clothing did not differ in its richness. His trousers bore the stamp of time: the light, bright green

15 Finnish—at that time, Finland was exporting a lot of clothing to the Soviet Union.

colors made by Azerbaijan craftsmen. Externally, they looked exactly like the foreign models.

The walk started. Or, it would be more correct to say, Janna and Serge crawled into every open door. It didn't matter if it was a store, or a café, or just simply a place to munch. When they came to a clothing store, they just looked at the togs. But from all the ice cream and soda water they consumed, by the end of Deribasovskia Street, their stomachs were truly thoroughly bloated. But they had to do this to drink and get cool, anyway: the scorching walls of the houses breathed out heat.

On both sides of the street neon fires shone. Multi-colored patches of light lay on the roadway. They lit up the laughing faces of walkers. Their bright outfits, with a range of colors, rippled in the eyes. From the nearest small restaurant, a noisy band of students ran out. Girls flashed bronze legs. The young men, who were a little tipsy, tried to get into the middle of the female bodies, which radiated with health. One blonde diligently shook her head, knowing that her soft wavy hair moved in different directions... This action deeply moved a guy who painfully wished to kiss her, but each time he tried, he came across a dexterously placed little elbow.

Serge passionately wanted to be with them. He also wanted to chase girls, embrace them, shout nonsense related to someone, it didn't matter to whom ...

Noticing this, Janna pulled him into a café, where behind little tables people drank cocktails from straws. Serge ordered two glasses and quickly drained his, placing the straw aside.

Having satisfied his thirst, they continued their voyage, but noticed the weariness that landed them in a cafe at a low, greasy, little table. In a corner, four fairly sloshed musicians vainly tried to portray something like a slow foxtrot. Lamps shone at full power, punching through the thick veil of cigarette smoke. It was somehow uncomfortable, not to mention nasty. Nevertheless, in the establishment almost all the little tables were full. Near the stage, the dancers were crowded on a narrow dance floor, trying to catch some satisfaction. Janna and Serge sat down against each other. Since it was more difficult not to smoke, they silently took a cigarette. Soon a depressing steak with an egg appeared on their table. Serge slowly thrust his cigarette butt in the ashtray and seized his fork ...

"Oh! Hello! Glad to see you!" Serge, in surprise, put his fork back down. Janna cheerfully waved her hand, since trying to overcome the noise in the hall was hopeless. In the adjacent hall there was a young man, rather decently dressed in an ironed jacket and tie. He stood with an unperturbed quiet demeanor and looked for a spot. At the same moment, he saw Janna shouting for some reason in English. His face blurred into a white-toothed smile, and he began to make his way to the little table. Serge noticed the intellectual was accompanied by a girl, who was obediently following him. The guy had an open and impudent face, open because it did not hide its impudence. His fast brown eyes caustically and keenly ran from object to object. His whole demeanor brazenly let everyone know that he was the cock of the walk.

"What brings you here, Valera! Why are you suddenly in Odessa?"

"Yes Jannochka.[16] It is a small world. You should have asked, though, why suddenly in this tavern?" said Valera, looking around in disgust.

"Have you been gone from Kishinev for a long time?"— Janna decided to pepper him with questions. "By the way,

---

16 Jannochka—term of endearment for Janna's name.

get acquainted with my groom, Seriozha,"[17] Janna pointed to Serge. Valera nodded and royally stretched out his hand. Serge languidly reached out his own, considering Janna's words. Valera lost no time to introduce his own *sputnik*. He called her Mila, and became occupied in conversation with Janna.

"Don't you know? I was on a business trip in the GDR.[18] I became exhausted—what a horror. So, I am here on a cultural vacation. By the way, I am also going to marry—her." Valera nodded in Mila's direction. She modestly smiled and bashfully looked away.

"Why are you eating dry food?" he continued. "Really, don't you have enough for a glass of wine? Well, I'll treat you ..."

After a while, on the table, there appeared bottles and every possible snack. Valera, probably, decided to impress everyone with his largesse. He pulled out a thick wallet and paid for the wine, for the steak, and for a tip for the waiter. He did all of this in such a way that it seemed that he would start to pay for the table next to them. He liked to be the center of attention and did not hide it. The conversation with Janna dove into Kishinev life like a spoon into porridge. There was little to understand, and to Serge, it was uninteresting. Mila did not participate in the conversation either, and slowly sipped from her glass. She was a very timid girl.

Her transparent eyes were gentle and tender. She could not bear direct eye contact and hastily lowered her eyelids. She tried to thank someone, when that person was only about to do a favor. It was the embodiment of femininity, charming, but still childish. She was studying at ballet school.

---

17 Seriozha— term of endearment for the name Sergey.
18 GDR—German Democratic Republic, also known as East Germany.

Exchanging short phrases with Mila, Serge secretly sneaked a look at Janna. "Why did she talk about a groom? Did she simply say these words, or was there some deeper meaning behind it? This phrase could prevent unwanted attention from Valera. But what for? Valera is with a lady. Did her words just tumble out? Then she has it on her mind. She wanted me to think about it. So, she achieved what she wanted: I am thinking about it. Although nothing similar came into my head until now. The bride, ha! What nonsense!"

Janna and Valera debated with fervency about the behavior of a mutual friend. Janna often switched into English, which surprised and intrigued Serge. Knowledge of foreign languages by someone in the USSR was more often the exception, rather than the rule. Only lucky people were going abroad, but mostly to other socialist countries. About the capitalist countries, mere mortals did not even dream. To meet foreigners and make friends with them was not only welcomed, but was even pursued. Yet to do this was dangerous. Why would you study languages? Where is the incentive? In any case, the people who surrounded Serge, both at school and at the institute, had no desire to study English or German. French, Spanish and other languages, were considered exotic, in general. Under these circumstances, a person knowing more than one language gained esteem with anyone who came in contact with them. The image of such a person automatically rose. And, as Serge discovered, his newly-made friend was such a person: without any effort, she threw out English phrases that Serge could not understand. An inexplicable feeling of pride was forming, but it was immediately superseded by the sensation of a growing abyss between him and this woman. "Who am I for her? Her future husband? Baloney!

What a milk sucker, what a greenhorn. Kisses are the only thing that she will allow you. You are simply a toy. She enjoys the opportunity to possess a lad, drowning in his sexual saliva. Maybe, she will allow herself to be close with you, for the sake of novelty sensations. But with this, her interest will end. What kind of a groom? Why did she say that?"

In the café, the wine had gone to Valera's head, and finding himself in the street, he became adventurous.

"So, let's go to a wonderful place I know. Quiet, no objections." He ran across the street, and reigned in a taxi like a lathered horse. Valera hoisted himself in the front seat, and in the voice of a minister named the address. In the car, he sat half-turned around, and entertained the ladies with secular chatter. Mila perched like a kitty cat between Serge and Janna, laughing at the tricks of her future groom, and Serge could not understand what attracted her to this boaster.

The taxi drove to the harbor. It is one of the architectural masterpieces of mature socialism. But it was not love of architecture that attracted the adventure seekers here. On the second floor, behind the windows covered with curtains, existed the world where our heroes aspired to go. It was a well-known restaurant of the harbor. Actually, it was well-known, because reservations were impossible to get. In each city, there are many such fashionable restaurants, with high demand because the public made them so popular.

Of course, there were no seats available. The forcefulness of Valera opening his wallet changed nothing. They could only reach one possible agreement: the door-keeper would bring them a couple bottles of wine. They had to be satisfied with only these, though Serge was not upset. He was only upset with the prolonged company of Valera.

They went down to the pier. The night was warm and quiet. It smelled of the sea, with anchor ropes, and crude oil. Cutters, barges, tugboats, walking ships—the small and big fleet shone with signal lights, and the long light beams bounced above the water, as they shuddered and vibrated from the ripples. The lungs greedily sucked in the damp air. One's chest breathed easily and freely, enjoying the smells of a powerful port.

"Hey, Serge, have a drink." Valera pushed him sideways and handed him the uncorked bottle. Serge took a couple of swigs and started the jug around the circle. In a minute, the bottle came around again and appeared in his hands. He took a sip and put it down on the still warm stones of the pier. He became tired of standing and sat down on the pilings. It seemed Janna and Valera had not seen each other since the birth of the Christ. They briskly discussed everything. Mila stood at some distance, and then joined Serge. He silently handed her the bottle. She tasted it and gave the wine back. Serge turned the bottle towards himself, and understood that there was nothing left to share. He poured the warm contents into his stomach.

Suddenly, a sharp noise came from above them. On the terrace of the restaurant, a carousing couple ran out. The woman, tearing the silence with squeaky laughter, tried to be rescued from a guffawing drunken hog. He opened his arms, and tried to catch his naughty girl. At last, he succeeded. Perhaps because his inhibitions had been replaced by vodka or because he had a lot of passion for her, he leaned on her with all his mass, pushed her to the handrail, and began to squeeze and slobber on her with such impatience, that soon her dress split, and the seam of her sleeve tore apart. This abruptly changed her mood. She pulled away and delivered a weighty slap in the face. The slap resounded like an echo, and she hurried to disappear through the doors. The man pondered what happened for a minute or two, leaned on the rails and began to spit in the water. Then he noticed the group of people on the pier and whistled.

"Hey you, on the pier, treat me with a cigarette." And he came downstairs, reeling from side-to-side.

"Don't bother. We don't have more cigarettes," shouted Valera.

"Ayyyy, I don't believe you. People like you can't be out of cigarettes. Let's have a drink." The man was almost next to them. Valera took a step towards him and started barking at him like a pug dog, wanting to prove that the guy didn't need to drink any more. He told him, "Go back to your company."

"I will still be in good time for my company," the good-natured lout put his weighty hand on Valera's shoulder. But suddenly, with a wrestling move, Valera removed the hog's hand and jumped aside, holding his fists at the ready.

The drunkard began to blink rapidly and said, "Hey dude, you shouldn't have done that. Now you fucked up." The man got ready to pound Valera, who was half his size. This business was taking an unpleasant turn. Serge got up, took an empty bottle, and broke it on the asphalt between the two fighters.

"This is over, guys! Hey buddy, people are getting tired of waiting for you. And we have some business to do too." Serge turned Valera around and nudged his back between his shoulders. Not looking back, the four trudged away.

Soon they forgot about the incident. They came close to Potemkin's Stairs.[19] Here Valera had a brainstorm. He picked up Janna and carried her up the stairs. On the first

---

19 The Potemkin Stairs is a giant stairway in Odessa, Ukraine and the best known symbol of Odessa. The stairs are considered a formal entrance into the city from the direction of the sea.

platform, he stopped and shouted, "Hey, who wants to go higher? Get her!" He nodded towards Mila. One must be an idiot to walk up the stairs, particularly Potemkin's Stairs, and particularly with a woman in his arms and on cotton legs, tired out from the whole day. But the intoxicated mind can barely think, and Serge swept up Mila. She was really light, like a ballerina, but this was enough. His wine-weakened muscles behaved horribly. Serge walked a flight with difficulty and, afraid that his heart would jump out of his chest, he lowered Mila down. Valera, in the meantime, ascended another two flights and guffawed victoriously.

Mila rose on tiptoe and touched Serge's hot cheek with her lips. "Thank you," she said, and easily climbed upward. They climbed to the platform where Valera and Janna stood.

"I knew you would lose," said Valera. "When you carried Janna over the street, your spine was caved in, and I understood that you are not as strong as you seem ..."

"Valera, when you went to the GDR did you hit your head somewhere?" asked Serge, and he moved further up the stairs.

"Maybe we will fight!" shouted Valera, but Serge did not stop. There was no rage in him, and there was no desire to fight. "So, the friends have showed up," he thought. "Some George, not from this world. And this one, looking like someone hit him from around the corner with a big sack. I wonder, are all her friends like this?"

The Stairs, at last, ended. Valera and Janna passed by, and Janna tried to calm her friend who had behaved like a rooster in a henhouse. Mila caught up with Serge, and they walked together. Serge was silent. Mila was also silent. Mila was lamb-like and quietly walked along the side, as if she was afraid to remind anyone of her presence. Serge did not care for this type of woman, but now she seemed pleasant to him. He discreetly looked at her. She smoothly moved her tiny legs, and occasionally slid her finger against the glass of shop-windows. In this moment, there was so much charm in her that Serge could not bear it, he stepped towards her, put his hands on her shoulders and touched her damp lips. She shuddered with unexpectedness, but when Serge tried to kiss her once again, she moved her palm in front of her mouth and whispered, "It is not necessary." She gave a look in the direction of Valera and noticed the significant distance. Serge wanted to embrace Mila, to pull her around a corner and join hands and quicken their pace without turning back, washing off these adult and complex beings who were somewhere ahead solving world problems.

On one of streets, the couples separated. Valera kissed Janna on the cheek and in exchange received the same ritual kiss. He did not even look at Serge. Having put his wide palm with short fingers on Mila's back, he walked away. From behind, it seemed that he carried her, grabbing her by the scruff of the neck. Mila next to him was a thing, a jacket thrown over an arm: when it is needed, he will put it on, but for the moment, he lets it dangle ...

Serge sourly watched them leave, turned away, and sighed deeply. He thought that he had the same role in their relationship with Janna. He turned and point-blank looked at his sputnik. She lowered her eyes.

"You know, I do not love such characters either. His father is a big shot, so he raised him that way... You understand. He even sent him to the GDR, for an internship."

"That's all right, enough of Valera. However, you were talking so affably with him."

"But he is always really nice to me. By the way, he has a lot of opportunities. His daddy paves the way for him."

"That means his daddy is *nuzhnik*.[20] Understood. Well, where shall we go?"

"For the moment, nowhere. Kiss me!" They kissed, then once again, and again. Valera, and Mila with him, promptly dissolved into nonexistence ...

It was long past midnight, after they'd wandered the streets of the falling-asleep Odessa, when they sat down on a small narrow bench on a lonely side street. The dark green mass of the trees completely hid them from the light of the lanterns. Janna stretched her legs, playing with the tips of her shoes. Her feet were small, not matching her height, which gave an aristocratic flair to the line of her foot. The miniature shoe and thin ankle would look graceful from under the folds of a long dress at some ball, a hundred and fifty years ago. A tall, shapely figure with a deep décolleté would be irresistible. Languid eyes and a wide, white-toothed smile would battle any suitor on the spot. Serge imagined himself as the duelist shooting away each contender. The right to possess such a woman is not cheap, and it is necessary to work hard to receive this right.

"This is my groom!" The phrase rung like a bell and was echoing in his brain. What drivel! The thin young man with long yellow hair looked like a chick that just hatched from an egg. He jumped a little bit around and landed in the embrace of a magnificent lady. And turned into her husband! It was simply a fairy tale about Ivanushka-Durachok.[21] Serge clapped his knees, then got up and started walking back and forth. He was going to tell her

---

20 Nuzhnik—Russian slang—in this case the word means the one who is needed. The word had a double meaning: in the past the word meant a toilet. The youth converted the word to mean needed, but like a toilet. A toilet is needed, but it is not the most pleasant analogy. It is a more derogatory term.
21 Ivanushka-Durachok — Ivan the Fool, who married a princess, is one of the best-loved heroes of Russian fairytales.

that he felt very good with her, and that he had no desire to separate from her now, or in the future. He considered that spending two days with such a girl was already a great success in his life. He was glad and, maybe even happy, though he imagined poorly what it meant to be happy with a woman. He was grateful to her ... But instead of telling her all this, he told an absurd joke about a flock of metal files which flew to the South, and one did not make it because it had no handles. Then he told her about the crocodile that crept over the railroad tracks. A train ran over him and the crocodile ascertained that his butt already arrived. Then Serge understood that he would not say anything about his confused feelings to her. And what for? The night was young, and he could kiss the chic young lady next to him if he wanted to—and if he didn't, then he wouldn't. Enjoy the moment—it may disappear. Why stir yourself up with vast reflections? Are you feeling good?—Good!

There comes such an easygoing feeling, and not because you are in love and you have love in return, but because you are not burdened with anything. The brain is free from cares. And you too are free, and you can choose to leave at any minute. And you can choose to stay ...

Serge remained. Like a cavalryman, he straddled a bench and... My God! His excellent Azerbaijan trousers burst directly on the seam, actually splitting his trousers into two pants legs. Janna, hearing the sound of ripping fabric, roared with laughter. And when Serge showed her the ripped butt, she slipped off the bench, and filled the silence with loud laughter. Laughing, they tied her suede handbag to his waist so that it hung behind and covered the breach.

Certainly, to dawdle in the streets in such attire was not desirable. Serge looked at the time, and it was half past two in the morning.

"Do you intend to go to your George?"

"Why not?"

"So do you feel like going there?"

"No. What are you offering?"

"To go to my place."

"Then, let's go ..."

Serge was stupefied. Actually, he did not count on such an answer, and now the thoughts in his head were chasing and replacing each other: night, a bed, a sofa, two rooms. In one room, his cousin slept with a child. In another one—him. There was one bed, and on it he slept—that means ...

They stood at a dark entrance, and Serge, thief-like, slowly opened the doors. In the apartment, there was a dead silence. The only sound came from the kitchen faucet, where water dripped like the ticking of a water clock. On tiptoe Serge made his way to his room, through it—to the room of his cousin and approached her peacefully snuffling body. He put a hand on her shoulder and shook her gently. His cousin woke up.

"What do you need?" she asked in a whisper.

"Excuse me, I am with a girl. Would you obje ..."

"Here, take the pillow from the armchair."

"What for?"

"Because there is only one there."

Serge was dumbfounded and stared into his cousin's face, which was dimly lit by a street lantern.

"But ..."

"Then take a folding bed."

"Yes, OK."

"Let it stand in its own place," thought Serge, and he quietly slipped through the door.

"You will sleep here." He brought Janna to a trestle bed standing in a corner. "Settle down. The bathroom is next to the kitchen. Let's go, I will show you, because you won't find it."

"Let go, I'm bright."

Talking in whispers, they crept into the kitchen. Serge got a piece of kielbasa from the refrigerator, found the bread, and divided it into two parts. She greedily attacked the meal and sat down on the edge of a stool. With full mouths, they tried to communicate somehow, but instead of words, only crumbs and suppressed laughter came out. Once done with the meal, Serge wiped his lips with his palm and plodded away to make the bed ...

Janna was already lying down when Serge approached and kissed her. The warm female scent tickled his nose and forced him to sit down beside her.

"Your cousin knows that I'm here?"

"She knows."

"And what does she say?"

"Nothing, everything is all right, sleep easy."

"And you?"

Instead of an answer, Serge embraced her and clung to her full sensual lips. They shuddered and slightly opened. From each touch, they swelled and breathed with heat, but her breath was deep and even. It seemed as if she knew that now it should happen, and waited for it, not with submissiveness, but with determined resoluteness. Serge began to shower her with kisses, enjoying her pliable, damp body. The blanket stirred, and he threw it on her legs. Janna immediately clasped his neck and pressed him to herself. Serge felt her breast rise like a wave and buried his face in the hollow between her two spheres. The smell of her sun-kissed skin made his head spin. His lips caressed the curve of her breast. They came across her firm, pointed nipple. He grabbed it with his teeth and gently pressed it. Suddenly, he heard a firm whispered, "Go, your cousin!.."

Serge got up, covered her with a blanket, wished her good night, and disappeared behind a door ...

When he lay on the folding bed, he thought, "You need to love a woman very much in order to overcome such a perfect opening," and he plunged into the dream of a righteous person.

***

Several days passed. Janna was going home. They sat at the buffet at the railway station, slowly sucking down warm coffee.

"It is only six days since we met, and it seems like an eternity has passed." Janna's voice sounded sad. She rotated the teaspoon in the glass, and spoke more to herself than to Serge.

"I will leave, and you, probably, will go to the beach and get acquainted with some other girl."

"Possibly." Serge grinned, trying to give the word a playful tone.

"We'll depart and will never meet again."

And this, to tell the truth, was not what Serge desired.

"Why? You in fact often visit Moscow."

"No, Serge, in Moscow we will not meet."

"I do not understand, what can prevent us meeting?"

"Hell knows what she was hammering into her head. Actually, if we won't meet, then we won't meet ..."

At this moment Serge thought that he was trying to convince himself. He filled himself with indifference, though he was actually very melancholy that she was leaving. And this melancholy would develop in full force when the train dragged her to Kishinev. But, he would remain on the platform by himself, without her, and would slowly go out in the now deserted city because for the entire six days in Odessa there was *She*, who filled the whole world with herself.

"What is the time?" Janna was obviously nervous.

"Almost an hour until departure."

"Do you have any cigarettes?"

"Yes, but smoking is not allowed here."

They went to the station building and sat down on a bench. Janna inhaled deeply; her look was thoughtful and serious ...

"Listen!" Suddenly, her eyes lit up. She became animated, and she began to glow from the idea that came into her mind.

"You come with me!"

"Did you think this through?"

"It's not important. You will come with me and that's it!"

"My things are not packed. My family will worry. Soon my parents will arrive," reasoned Serge.

"This is not a problem." Janna did not give value to his words. "You will send a telegram. You will calm them down. You will spend two or three days and leave. You will see Kishinev."

"What does Kishinev have to do with this? What a reason ..." thought Serge.

"And your mom, when does she arrive?"

"Mom?" Janna rummaged in her memory. "On the third, or the fourth. She will also call on her friends. In any case, I'm going to buy a ticket."

"Wait, where will I go in these clothes?"

Serge pointed at his shabby jeans.

"And the money that I have with me—it's only three rubles."

"Money, we will get there. I should receive an advance payment."

"But I need to take something with me," protested Serge.

Janna looked at the face of the clock.

"There are thirty-five more minutes. We'll take a taxi, we'll be on time."

She jumped to her feet. Her fervor carried her away. Serge began to consider an excursion to Moladavia, but the voice of common sense kept him back. In truth, it gradually faded, being replaced by the spirit of an adventurous undertaking. Janna waited, frozen in front of him. He looked at her widely spread, straight legs, raised his eyes to her firm hips, then above—to her chest heaving from impatience. Then his eyes slipped to her long gentle neck, and for a second, stopped on her full, compressed, sharply outlined lips—and at last, met her eyes which had become greener from an internal pressure. In them, there was a mix of despair, determination, and entreaty, and the multitude of feelings were now turbulent in her heart. "Perhaps, if I was only a toy, she would not look like this. To be with this woman, even for two or three more days. Ahh, why am I sitting? Fool!" Serge imagined Janna's empty house ... and jumped from his spot. They rushed to a taxi, and in half an hour were at the station again. The train departed in four minutes. Serge held a small bag in his hands where he had put his trousers and a second shirt. In three days, he intended to return, just before the arrival of his parents. But then he did not yet know that the passion to travel would fundamentally change the rest of his life.

***

The old man took a swig from a bottle of water. Then he bent and moistened his gray-haired balding head. Then, he got more comfortable on the boat's bench and looked at the sky. The sun still was high in the sky. In a few more hours, it would bend around the earth, slowly releasing its place to darkness.

It is strange how one moment can change your whole life. The old man thumbed through the pages of his own life, flying through the years. He suddenly remembered how he skidded on a spring road[22] and the helpless car pulled directly towards a quickly moving truck. At the last second, he plowed into a snowdrift on the roadside, and the multi-ton truck swept past, the driver gesturing crazily and growling the engine. Serge was lucky to survive. He got lucky once more when a car driving in front of him suddenly made a U-turn and ran sideways into a pickup truck. The car smashed its front-end into a safety barrier, and passers-by had to pull out the blood-stained bodies of the young guys still writhing in agony. In one instant, everything grew dim. What if the pickup had not been there?

But if Serge remained on the platform, and watched the train leave, everything would be different. How? Nobody knows how. Different, that's all. Nevertheless, they lodged in the train car together, across from each other. The train squeaked with all its wheels and it rolled them into a life full of riddles, many of which the old man could not solve in the years that followed.

* * *

---

22 Spring road—in Russia, winters are long and the snow lasts long into the spring.

The train was a suburban type with bench seats. There were not many passengers sitting there. At once, you could smell kielbasa, boiled eggs, fresh cucumbers and other food. To fill your stomach while on the road is a ritual action impossible to remove. Like before travel time, everybody was painfully starved.

For Serge and Janna, though, no supplies existed, and contrary to their custom of eating, they expected a forced three-hour fast. As if to spite them, a well-fed man sitting beside them tried to fill his chubby boy with cutlets.[23] The boy shook his head side-to-side like a brat, and the man, not getting upset, placed the next piece into his own mouth. Janna and Serge had no strength to observe this procedure for long, so they went to the end of the train car. Wheels were tapping out kilometers. Serge leaned against a shaking wall and smoked. Janna stood opposite. Her face was concentrated, and her brow was furrowed. She looked very adult, and to Serge communication with this woman seemed ridiculous. What forces prompted him to go with her now? Far from places he had known and held dear, and in the end, far from his favorite sea. He goes to strangers, with another stranger, in effect, a strange woman. "Who is she to me? Who is she in at all?" thought Serge, glancing at his sputnik. Janna slowly lifted her eyelashes. Her sight was tired, but not full of pity. It belonged to a woman used to exhaustion, struggling and winning. To tell the truth, at that moment, Serge did not yet understand this. He followed his natural instinct instead, not being able to separate from his object of desire. He was ruled by unsatisfied passion. He did not look any further at the impending night. How could he know that Janna already separated from him, and looked into the far future?

---

23 Cutlets—Russian hamburgers.

They returned to their seats and asked the big man for his copy of *Ogoniok*.[24] He gladly gave them the magazine, mainly because he did not know what to do with it. Janna found a long article about Delacroix and started to read aloud. Serge listened. But her voice hardly reached through the noise of the moving train. So as not to lose the idea, he began to read it himself, and successfully reached the end of the article, but still did not comprehend the entire plot. Janna understood it, and began to explain conscientiously to Serge that Delacroix represented a chapter of the Romantic movement in painting. Popularity came to him in 1822, when he exhibited the large painting *Barque of Dante* at a Parisian salon. He was the master of the color scale and influenced Renoir and Van Gogh ... Serge listened, but only understood one thing: that to become infatuated with art, it is necessary to try to absorb art into yourself. To feel it, not in the mind, but in the heart. But this can't be done on a train.

He played along by dropping general phrases, and then dipped into vast demagogy about how your profession influences the formation of your worldview. Janna said that there are certain important things, and not to know about them is simply impossible, no matter what a person is engaged in. Serge felt reproached, became isolated, and went the rest of the way in silence. He tried to justify his ignorance somehow, but unfortunately, could not.

* * *

Around ten o'clock in the evening the electric train brakes began to squeal in the capital of Moldavia.

---

24 Ogoniok—Russian "Spark" magazine.

The weather was excellent. Warm evening air filled the lungs, and the smell of summer was striking the nostrils. People tumbled out of the station, dragging backpacks and suitcases with different belongings inside. The crowd was forming lines, but the approaching trolley buses cut pieces off, and carried them into the city.

Janna certainly wished to go by taxi. But the line for a taxi was long too, and to wait for a long time could not be helped ... until they noticed Valera. He stood at the front of a line. Janna, with her characteristic ability to never miss a moment, rushed towards him.

Valera, having seen Serge, was not as glad for this meeting. But, he gave them a lift to the house, naturally at his expense with undisguised arrogance.

"Isn't Valera a sweetheart, even though he has some eccentricities?" Janna said when they left the car. But Serge didn't care: Valera was uninteresting to him. Much later he learned of Valera's untimely death from an overdose of drugs ...

Janna's habitation[25] was a small one-story house on a scrap of ground. Small fruit trees, currant bushes, and some other vegetation grew around. However, no one tended to it, and it was given over to the arbitrariness of destiny. A lop-sided gate with a rattling chain closed the entrance to the yard. From the windows of her hut, light streamed, and with the clink of the chain, an elderly woman came out. Serge understood that this was Janna's mother. Mom had a loud, hoarse voice. She was not able to speak quietly or slowly. As soon as she saw her daughter, the garden was filled with enthusiastic exclamations. From depths of the foyer came one more character—a thin girl. She began to jump around Janna (who towered above her),

---

25 Habitation—In the Soviet republic of Moldavia, the climate was warm with lots of sunshine, so it was crowded. After WWII, housing was scarce.

trying to hang on her neck. Serge appeared to be forgotten and, remaining in the shadow of the trees, observed the greeting scene. At last, it was his turn, and he was presented as George's cousin—the inveterate tourist who needed to get familiar with the capital of Moldavia.

After that, Serge was forgotten again, and left to himself.

From nowhere visitors began to arrive. They came in pairs, or alone, and soon the small room became crowded. Not to cause a commotion, Serge nested in a corner. He put an absent look on his face, but kept an interested eye on everything. By their appearance, the way they behaved, and their conversations, the people were local bohemians. They were talking about the cinema, news, theatre, who arrived where, who they met, what was new in the philharmonic society, and so many other things. Serge didn't have the slightest clue about what they were talking about and was afraid that they would ask his opinion.

Mother rattled saucepans in the kitchen, someone helped her, and from there fragments of phrases and laughter filled the air. This pandemonium worked unpleasantly on Serge. He had counted on silence, a wide bed, and Janna's closeness. He felt tired, broken, and terribly hungry.

At last, in the chaos, some organization started to loom. On the table, products of culinary art began to appear: fried eggs with bacon, cut sausage, bread, and ... a decanter with vodka. Serge was not attracted to the vodka, but he could eat all the food by himself. He became gloomy that he needed to share with everyone. However, the bohemians considered eating a lot of food plebeian and Serge had an opportunity to snatch a bigger piece, but the alcohol (in the bottle there was pure, high-proof alcohol) was gloriously consumed by them.

They also poured for Serge. The alcohol burned his mucous membranes, choked his throat, and the company became repugnant to him. He swallowed often, trying to rescue his throat, but nothing helped, and tears welled up in his eyes. To hide his indisposition, he left for the porch and lit a cigarette. A thin chatterbox ran out to him, and started to shower him with questions: "Who are you? Where are you from? Why are you with Janna? What is your relationship?" Serge answered evasively. He had a devilish desire to send her to hell, but did not want to insult her. However, all this receded into the background, because as the nausea was driving up his throat, his language dried up, and his only thought was how to keep from vomiting.

It was already late. The "high society" poured into the courtyard and intended to leave for their homes. Janna spun among them. She listened and spread compliments, and kissed everyone at parting. When the crowd was past the gate, Serge looked with disgust at the narrow-shouldered, deformed figures of the "patrons of art" and spit between his legs. Janna stood at the gate and exchanged a few last sentimental phrases. Serge switched his view to her bronze legs which had been snatched out from the darkness by a shaft of door light, and with a malicious greed wanted her. He imagined how he would sadistically seize her, but immediately dropped this idea because her mother appeared on the threshold.

"Janna, are you smoking?" she cried out.

"No, Mom."

"Watch it, do not smoke. I am going to sleep." At last, Janna remembered about Serge and sat down on his lap.

"Give me a cigarette."

"Take one." Serge leaned on the warm wall of the house. Janna took a drag.

"How do you like my friends?"

"So-so, I didn't get a taste."

"They are charming. True?"

"Maybe."

"Kiss me."

"I don't want to."

"Kiss me, I said!" She imperiously looked at him and pouted with her lush lips.

Serge touched them.

"You are able to kiss better." She tenderly leaned towards him.

"Well kiss me, your lips are so soft." Serge felt like some narcotic substance went to his legs, and rose up higher, into his head. He embraced her ...

"Behind the house, in the garden, there is a bed. I will go and get a mattress..." Janna whispered to his face.

"Here it comes. She is mine. Now she does not lie, she really wants it." It seemed to Serge, that this already happened some time ago, and that it occurs every day, and here again he would be in bed with a woman, so close and so familiar ...

Janna came out, covered by a mattress, a blanket and pillows.

The bed was narrow, rusty, and had a sagging grid. They sat down on the edge, not daring to start for the sake of what they came here to do. Through the half-naked garden the street was visible, and shadows of passers-by occasionally flashed. Serge wearily tumbled down on the pillows and closed his eyes. He was not rushing. But weariness prevailed. Falling asleep, he felt a descending weight. The bed took the form of a hammock, and it became very uncomfortable. Serge tried to move, but the bed was too narrow. Janna seemed to be very heavy and inappropriate in the hanging space. He wanted to push her out from here and plunge into a sweet dream. But his desire from all the previous days woke up his body. Serge took off his shirt, threw off his trousers and covered himself with a thick blanket. Janna immediately pressed him to herself. She had wide hips, and she easily accepted him. She quietly and languidly waited, for the time when he would do what he so aspired to all these days. Serge tried to stir her, to excite reciprocal passion, but he lost control. From his throat, a hoarse groan was pulled out. The delightful wave lifted him, with a violent forceful whirlwind, immersing him in an abyss, and then rolled away leaving him, soft, exhausted, and barely trembling ...

The breeze rustled through the leaves. On the ground the first yellow leaflets silently fell. Autumn was coming ...

***

Time flew imperceptibly. They left behind not only three days, but ten days. It was difficult for Serge to watch the days fly by, and he didn't even want to do this—he did not want to leave this carefree life, and there was no reason to speed it up.

Every morning, half asleep, but pretending to be deeply sleeping, Serge waited, laying on his folding bed until the time when her mother would leave the house and go to work. The gate chain was a signal: as soon as its clanking became silent, Janna's imperious voice called to the sleeper and Serge moved from the narrow creaking folding bed to Janna's wide and soft bed. They seldom rose until lunch. Only the unique force of famine was able to unclench their embrace. Getting up was always difficult and undesirable. Janna usually rose first, and spent a long time in the house, flaunting Eve's suit, unwillingly leaving Serge's warmth, but also his sight.

She usually finished putting on makeup and getting ready in about an hour, dressed in clothes, and only then was allowed in the street. At that point, the idea of a meal completely owned Serge. He hastened to put on his clothes, and together, they went out to dine. Sitting down at a convenient little table, they ordered so much food that to eat it all was practically impossible. They became drowsy from the meal and carried their bodies to a small park where they sat full and happy, gradually talking about everything.

By the evening, they again found the ability to move and went to the lake, or to the cinema, or simply wandered on the streets depending on their mood.

Their stormy life began later, closer to the night when a normal Soviet worker gets in a hurry to depart to a dream. The nightlife of our heroes was filled with table-talks with Janna's friends about literature and art. When the attraction to beauty was increased by doses of strong drink, Serge would lose the context of the discussions. But he felt some falseness when everyone sitting around had such smart looks on their faces; it was a disgrace to look that clever when everyone considered themselves an expert in almost everything and with full competence expressed their thoughts on things when they didn't have the foggiest notion.

Once they were invited by a musician for a cup of coffee and a pair of jazz records. The coffee was tasteless, the equipment magnificent, and the records incomprehensible. In a small room about ten people were placed—all of them passionate music fans. In the corners were hanging speakers. On the floor multi-colored wires that looked like worms crept about, and next to a window stood a second-hand

Yennika[26] electronic piano. On the old shabby sofa sat the owner, thin and long. His head was moderately shaking to the music on a lean neck. His eyes were closed and he rose into the world of sharps and flats, scales and chords, and from his temple the treble clef spread. His coffee cooled down—he had no time for coffee. It seemed that only he understood this set of sounds and derived pleasure. The others glanced at him with the same spiritualized look, but they did not forget to sip from their coffee cups.

Serge listened to the first side of the record, trying to get into its essence. The end of the second side—he waited with impatience. Brought up on heavy rock rising in popularity at that time, Serge did not care for any other music, just like his many peers—twenty-year-old playboys. All his friends were raised on Led Zeppelin, Deep Purple, and Slade, and none dared miss the rock opera *Jesus Christ Superstar*.

When the player started spinning one more record, Serge felt a loss of energy. Jazz—is a complex genre, and its circle of fans are able to hear something special that is not given to anyone else. It seemed, out of all the company, that only the host could be considered that type of person.

Serge caught Janna's eye, and they began to play 'viewers': the one who blinks first—loses. It seems, Janna won. After the click of the record player's self-locking device, she called everyone to judge who had longer lips, Serge or her. A school ruler appeared, and they began to measure. Janna's lips appeared to be longer.

The musician was praised for a miraculously spent evening, and the whole company moved to visit one more representative of beauty, a well–known sculpture artist. In her studio, there was a set of hand-made articles from

26 Yennika—Czech equipment.

clay, plaster, and stone. Everyone admired her talent, and admired the reproductions of painters, hanging on the walls. But, the table layout was the most interesting ...

Here too were fans of music, but as they had only started to love it, they only had one record. Through hissing and a crash the voice of Adamo reached them. It was discovered that everyone loved to dance, and Adamo had to work very hard, and for this everyone loved him too. Serge did not remember how he reached his folding bed. But he reached it, and this happened at daybreak ... the next day.

***

Serge woke up from conversation in an adjacent room.

"Janna, it seems to me that Serge is not George's cousin," said her mother. "He doesn't look like him at all."

Serge never even looked his 'cousin' in the eyes, but thought that her mother was absolutely right—Serge could not resemble George in any way.

"Who is he, Janna?"

"Yes, Mom, he is not George's cousin. But I love him and that makes it a good enough reason for him to be here."

"Is he a good person?"

"Yes, very much."

"You sure?"

"Mom, you ask too many questions. I want to sleep. I will tell you everything later."

"All right, I have to go. Today I will go to my sister's. Don't wait for me."

"That's good. When will you return?"

"Tomorrow evening or the day after tomorrow."

"All right, do not worry, Mom. Everything will be OK!"

The gate squeaked, and Serge got up from his saggy box on the floor.

"For two days we will be alone—Mom left for a visit," Janna whispered, kissing him. "And now we shall have a sleep. After yesterday, I am absolutely dead tired."

They embraced, and like children who tired themselves out by running, plunged into a deep dream.

Serge woke up first. Janna still slept, breathing deeply and evenly. He began to study her face as if he was looking at it for the first time. Her cute nose was somehow correctly attached. Her lips were full and bright without lipstick. Long eyelashes with mascara covered her eyes. Dark hair fell down on the pillow, and opened up to a high forehead with upturned eyebrows. Soft cheeks looked as if they were only intended for kisses.

"My God, this woman loves me! Have I misheard? Am I happy, or not yet? Maybe she just simply said so, for the sake of avoiding superfluous questions. Really. If I am not George's cousin and if she does not love me, then why the hell am I sticking around here?" He had to compose something. But to compose with a sleepy head, there was no desire. "Well, she said 'I love him'—What other questions can follow?"

Serge cautiously moved the blanket and barely uncovered Janna's breast, crowned with a beautiful brown nipple. He pulled the blanket a little more. The second breast came into view. They were like twins, forever joined in the middle. One came to an end, and at once another began, with the same beautiful, white skin as though the bathing suit kept them pristine.

Serge wanted to uncover her completely, but he was afraid that she would wake up. He cautiously pushed a hand under the blanket and put a palm on her stomach. Then he went further down and felt her soft hair ...

"Come to me," whispered Janna through her dream and Serge slowly, stretching out the pleasure, entered her.

"It feels like you are drinking me."

"And I thought the opposite—that I am giving you a drink."

"Today you are prohibited from satisfying my thirst—it's not the right time."

Suddenly, because of what he heard that morning, from the tender words she spoke, and the infinite fidelity where she gave him her body—Serge felt an inflow of such force that he barely had time to leave her warmth... He lay trembling on her in uncontrollable convulsions. Then he calmed down, barely rising on his elbows, and lowered his head to her breast. She smoothed and fingered his hair, calming him, and suddenly asked:

"Why don't you ever say anything, when you do it?"

"I don't know. It doesn't work simultaneously."

"You still never admitted you love me. Don't you love me?"

"Who can tell for certain? It can seem like love to that person."

Serge had read this phrase somewhere and quite agreed with the author.

"And what does it seem to you now?" Janna asked insistently.

"If I speak about this minute, it seems that I love you."

"And all other minutes and hours—you don't?!"

"This is not the right case to exercise logic."

"Then I will tell you directly and concretely: 'I love you, Serge.' I love without any 'it seems'!—Get up, I need to get a shower." She strongly pushed him away, jumped off the bed and escaped to the bathroom.

After a while, she returned, washed and refreshed. And like nothing happened, she said she was hungry and that Serge had to prepare twenty fried eggs.

Twenty—no, not twenty. About eight eggs were found in the refrigerator ...

They ate the sunny side up eggs, dipping their bread in the yolk and washing it down with milk.

"I have an idea!" Janna exclaimed. "We should go to a banya[27] today."

"That sounds like an excuse," answered Serge with words from a well known joke.[28]

"No, we need to steam and wash ourselves very well. I have such a necessity."

"I am not against that."

The Soviet banyas were segregated by sex because the communist power enforced the chastity of people of the highest social formation. The Russian banyas became a relic. They burned extremely hot while everyone washed simultaneously: men and women, adults and children. The Finnish traditions of unisex saunas, in general, remained in Finland.

Janna declared to the attendant that she was with her husband and thus it was not necessary to have a separate washing cabin. To Serge's surprise, the cabin was presented to them. They furiously rubbed each other with rigid sponges and with pleasure placed their backs under jets of

---

27 Banya—a communal-style or private rooms bathing house with hot steam.
28 The joke: "Let's go to the banya, and by the way, maybe we should wash ourselves.

hot water. Serge noticed a scar on her buttocks and asked where it came from.

"A dog bit me in childhood—does it bother you? Me, not at all. Now it will seem to you that you won't love me with a defect."

Instead of an answer, Serge embraced her, soapy and slippery, and kissed her on her wet lips.

"Oh you got scared! Fear not, there are no more defects!" She burst out laughing, and showed her healthy white teeth.

"Hey, newlyweds, time's up!" called the banya attendant at the door. "Others also need to wash themselves." The administrator did not lie; she spoke the naked truth. And soon, the heat-reddened and newly named 'married couple' Serge and Janna went outside, turning their faces to the warm, but still fresh wind.

They went into a cafe, and ate a sandwich with yesterday's cheese while they drank tea. They had no desire to wander around the city, or to fill the time by visiting someone either. They needed to use the free time given by her kind mom ...

"So, how do we look as newlyweds?" Janna asked, sitting down on the bed and folding her legs under her.

"I think, quite authentic."

"But in fact we are not newlyweds."

"Does that matter now?"

"In that case, why are we not newlyweds, if it doesn't matter?"

"That's not what I meant. We look like newlyweds, but it is nobody's business what we are in reality."

"We are newlyweds for kicks... Serge, marry me!"

He was taken aback. Her gaze was serious and she looked steadily at him. There was no reason to think that she was joking. Therefore, it seemed somehow frivolous to laugh the matter off.

"Do you want to become my wife?"

"Wouldn't you wish to have such a wife?"

"I did not think of it," Serge lied for some reason. "I feel good with you and in my opinion we are not going to part."

"You will leave soon."

"So what?"

"This means, that we will part."

"For some time—yes, but in fact not forever."

"It won't be like this, Seriozha. You will start your life. And I will continue to live mine. After a while, the need to meet will disappear."

Serge was not at all ready for such a conversation. He again studied her—to look at her was true pleasure. He remembered the morning closeness and decided that they needed to shift away from such a theme.

"You know," he said slowly, sitting down next to her on the bed, "I don't have anything at all against marrying you. More than that—I want this. But, let's agree. Today we decided to get married! And that's it. These are quite enough decisions for today. We will discuss the details another time. Does it work?"

"That's good. And when will the other time come?"

"Soon. Tomorrow, perhaps."

"Well, tomorrow we discuss details." She laughed and became clearly cheerful. "Hell, we should have a drink for this!"

But there was no drink, and Serge had to gallop to a shop that was already closing. Back then, by the rules of socialist service, ten minutes before a shop was closing, a worker stood next to the door and explained to everyone who was coming to the door that the shop was already closed. "We will finish servicing those who are inside!" the worker told him. Serge smiled sweetly, bent towards the saleswoman and explained that he was in the middle of getting engaged, and there was not enough wine for the guests ... Compassionately, she congratulated him and allowed him to come in through the door. "And why are you shoving? I told you, the shop is closed!" she yelled at the next person who tried to squeeze himself through the treasured door. Serge bought two bottles of Moldavian red wine. It seemed the evening promised not to be boring ...

When he returned, the table was laid out with cut tomatoes, cucumbers, onions, greenery, and two opened containers of canned fish. Janna was dressed for dinner, which is to say she removed all her clothes and threw a light robe over her naked body.

"Take off your clothes. It is hot!" she ordered. It was not necessary to persuade Serge. He quickly pulled off his trousers and ripped off his shirt, and remained in his underwear.

"I asked you to undress. Here, you see, this is how it needs to be." She opened her dressing gown, and stood before him in what she was born some time ago.

"Well. You will be in a dressing gown, and I will be stark naked. No, it won't work."

"And how will it go?" The dressing gown was thrown on the couch.

They opened a bottle and poured some wine.

"Let's have a toast," Janna offered, and they intertwined their arms in the manner of a bridal couple toasting each other. Then they began to kiss. Janna sprayed some wine into his mouth that she had not yet swallowed. He did the same and the sweet red jets dripped down their chins onto their naked bodies. The canned fish in a tomato sauce looked in surprise at these strange eaters, not understanding when it would be their turn. They poured another glass. Janna drank half, the rest splashed out on Serge's chest and she began to lick him.

"Did I choose a good way of consuming alcohol?"

"We need to patent it," answered Serge, trying to think up a sophisticated response. He wanted to break an egg on her stomach, but remembered that they ate all the eggs. Then he sat her on a chair. On her ears he hung the green onions, on her head he put parsley and celery, the tomatoes he spread over her breast, and in her mouth he thrust a cucumber. He stood to one side, evaluated her and pronounced: "You know, I had some doubts in the morning, but now, none at all. Only a fool would not marry such a bride."

Janna was lop-sided in the mirror. The cucumber jumped out of her mouth, she fell to her knees, and she could not overcome an attack of laughter. As always, she did not care how she looked when she laughed.

Then they grabbed the fish with their teeth, right out of the can, and fed each other. When the wine was finished, they ran out into the courtyard and began to pour water over each other from a hose, washing off the rest of their solemn supper ...

The first rays of the sun found them sleeping, barely covered by a bed sheet. The table looked as if it was ravaged the evening before by squad of hussars.[29] Married life began ...

"The husband, and the wife!" The newly-awake Janna sat on the bed and took a look at him with wide-open eyes. "You left your passport in Odessa."

---

29 Hussars—members of a European light cavalry unit.

"So what?"

"How will we submit the application for our marriage license?"

"We will submit it in Moscow. You are going to come there."

"In Moscow, it will take three months. Why should we lose that time? Collect yourself. We're going to the railway station."

"What for?"

"We'll set off for Odessa."

Serge began to strain his still sleepy head. He had no desire to be dragged somewhere.

"Now it is eight in the morning, and we will already be back here by the evening."

"Maybe she is right. To submit the documents for the license doesn't mean to marry yet. Still, there will be time to weigh it all out," thought Serge.

The taxi quickly brought them up to the station. But the train departed only in the middle of the day. It meant that it would not be possible to return today.

"We will go by taxi."

The long-distance taxi made trips from Kishinev to Odessa for twenty rubles. The driver carried four passengers, took from each of them five rubles, and barreled along for 170 kilometers.

"Why would you go, and spend extra money?" Serge tried to dissuade her. "I will go alone."

"And will you return?" Tears started forming in Janna's eyes.

"I promise."

They embraced, and Serge sat down in the front seat of the taxi.

The way was not the closest, but by the middle of the day Serge was back in his cousin's apartment.

"Your parents have arrived. They are staying at the dacha[30] with my mom. Will you meet them?" His cousin's voice had traces of disturbing notes.

"Yes. But in a couple of days. Now I have to go back, so we can submit the application to the Registry Office."[31]

"Why are you in such a hurry, Serge? This is not the way this kind of business is done."

"And how is it done? Like my father who waited for four years for my mother? No, it's not that time now."

There was no point in trying to persuade Serge. It seemed as if he had a horse's bridle in his mouth. And then, he promised Janna, his Janna, he would return today. Hastily saying goodbye, Serge hurried back on his way.

He did not take into account that as soon as he left the house of his cousin, she rushed off to the summer residence to tell his parents about Serge's plans. He did not know that, during the trip back to Kishinev, his parents already visited the militia and asked for their assistance to find their stray son. They needed to rescue their son—this was the goal that was standing in front of them with its full height. But the militia did not do anything. Serge was not missing in action, he was not killed, and no one was harming him. He was legally an adult, and went to his bride. The case was obviously not criminal—"deal with it yourself, friends," they said. For the poor parents, it only remained to wait, to see when and in what quality their offspring would again stand in front of their eyes.

***

---

30 Dacha—summer house.
31 Registry Office—where you submit applications for permission to marry and get married.

"I already agreed. The application will be accepted, but there is a chance to marry as well," said Janna.

Serge trusted poorly in this chance. The strict laws said: submit the application, think properly, and wait at least a month. Then, we will welcome you with Mendelssohn's wedding march.

But Janna thought differently. Her irrepressible energy carried her away to somewhere every morning. And in the evenings, she said that some 'channel' misfired, but that there were still other options left. If these do not turn out, they would submit the application the last day before Serge leaves.

Two days remained. For Serge, there was no doubt that all efforts for the marriage were in vain. Therefore, he easily passed the days in a hammock, read books which Janna insistently recommended to him, and waited for his fate. In effect, he lost nothing. His desire to marry this energetic woman only became stronger. She not only gave herself to him, but also carried him away into a whirlwind life, saturated with events. Gradually he got closer to her friends, and many of them appeared to be very colorful, interesting figures. They were intellectually developed people, knowledgeable and widely-read, and keen on world affairs. Around them, life was interesting.

The only thing that depressed Serge was that he could not support many conversations owing to his ignorance and the absence of the necessary knowledge. At school, he did not love literature. And who loved it—this state literature of the school program? Gorky's *Mother* and Tolstoy's *War and Peace* were inaccessible to the understanding of sixteen year-old kids. School literature beat off the desire to read. In due time, though, he consumed Hugo's *The Hunchback of Notre Dame* and *The Man Who Laughs*; read some Zola and Maupassant, and certainly, was in ecstasy from *The Three Musketeers*. To this, it was possible to add adventure books by Jules Verne, and detective stories...this, perhaps, was his baggage. Who spoke about such books at parties? Nobody. They discussed authors about whom Serge didn't even have a clue. They discussed novels and stories from thick literary magazines which he never held in his hands. What could he talk about? About theoretical mechanics, resistance of materials, higher mathematics—the subjects which he studied in the institute? Hardly. The initial courses of higher education were boring in the same way. Cheerful and uncomplicated parties had made up his previous life.

Serge hoped that with Janna's help he would quickly liquidate his ignorance. And when she gave him the next book, he tried not simply to read through it, but also to understand the sense which the author wished to convey to the reader. So, she imparted to him a love of Hemingway, speaking of him as the outstanding writer of the 20th century.

"Today you will read from here to here," Janna told him, having counted out about a hundred pages, as she rushed to leave for the last resolute attempt to marry. One day remained. Tomorrow Serge needed to leave—the new semester was starting, indicating that his vacation was over.

Serge lay in the hammock under the arches of the turning yellow garden and held in his hands a volume of Hemingway. The snows of Kilimanjaro were far away, and real life was near. "Will she succeed or not?" thought Serge, sliding his eyes over the lines ...

"Please don't talk that way. Couldn't I read to you?"

"Read what?"

"Anything in the book bag that we haven't read."

"I can't listen to it," he said. "Talking is the easiest. We quarrel and that makes the time pass."

"I don't quarrel. I never want to quarrel. Let's not quarrel any more. No matter how nervous we get. Maybe they will be back with another truck today. Maybe the plane will come."

"I don't want to move," the man said. "There is no sense in moving now except to make it easier for you."

"That's cowardly."

"Can't you let a man die as comfortably as he can without calling him names? What's the use of slanging me?"

"You're not going to die."

These were the words old man Hem wrote, though why he was called the old man was not clear. Having decided that in this world he already did his best, Hemingway died early, at only sixty-one, by thrusting a double-barreled gun into his mouth. "He was a strong person," thought Serge, though in his school electives, the class teacher insisted that suicide shows weakness of the spirit.

From a whiff of wind, yellow leaves were strewn, baring the branches of trees. Through them, the dark blue sky, of the still not interrupted summer was seen.

"You are not ready yet? Put on your clothes, we don't have much time." Janna flew into the garden. "There is a car outside, they are waiting for us." Like a tornado she slipped into the house. She ran out and threw Serge his clothes. Serge dropped out of the hammock, pulled on his trousers and put on a sleeveless jacket.

The car Janna hired was the last creation of the masters of Tolyatti.[32] Behind the wheel a man-bear, in some improbable way, found room for himself. "Bear" carried them to the restaurant where they were met by "the Grey Wolf". Lean, hungry, with burning eyes, he furiously filled his stomach, washing down the food with vodka.

The 'Wolf' was a procurer. He knew the brother of some sister who knew all the secret passages of the Wedding Palace. After "Bear" filled his belly with a couple shots of vodka, he again sat down behind the wheel. For a few hours, the poor car drove around different places where there were people who knew someone, who tried to help and sent them somewhere else. With each kilometer, the marriage mechanism grew; the flywheel was spinning. It seemed to Serge that from all these efforts, something would turn up. Every little screw of this mechanism represented a problem solver, who was an expert in this kind of enterprise. Serge was touched by their ability to give kind words, to promise, to call by phone, to agree and so on ... all without achieving the final result. This set of people was involved in the business campaign of Serge and Janna. With each person it was necessary to drink a glass of liquor—and one more, they said, for success. Serge with his natural adventurism started to like this process. He liked to get out of the car, with a purposeful and full of care look, talk in confidential meetings, open bottles, and end up with ... pockets full of addresses to follow up with other leads. The mechanism puffed, snuffled, creaked gears, trying with all its might; it was already impossible to stop it.

The car drove down a side street. The building of the bureau of the Registry Office flaunted itself on the right.

---

32 Tolyatti—city in Italy—naming the Italian & Russian produced cars.

On the left there was a strong point—the bunker—the house of an old school friend of Janna's, where everyone tumbled in, drunk from the drinks consumed that day. Serge was already slightly tipsy.

In the house they were celebrating a jubilee—the fifth birthday of the daughter of the school friend. The little girl had many adult admirers, and all of them tried to drink to the health of the child by which the child was quite satisfied. To Serge it seemed that it was just another party, and the closeness of the Registry Office was just a coincidence. Evening was coming. You could hardly expect that something would happen today. Serge relaxed, and sat down on a sofa. He leaned on the back of it and closed his eyes. He was covered at once by the wine drowsiness. The noise of the feast was fading...

Suddenly he was seized by the shoulders, and someone shook him like a guilty schoolboy.

Serge regained consciousness; in front of him stood Janna. "They will call us now. Put yourself in order."

"Where will they call?"

"You will see, let's go."

They went down to the street, crossed the road, and stood at the locked door of the opposite building. Suddenly Janna thought about something and ran back. Serge remained in a shadow of a huge poplar tree. The street was empty. The wind fingered the branches, and the ground was decorated with yellow-red leaves. On the bark of the tree, a beetle crept along tending to his affairs. The armor on it was black and gleamed with an emerald color. It came across the edge of the bark and waved its short antennae, not knowing where to move.

Serge's cheeks burned; his temples pounded. Someone invisible sat inside him and whispered, "Don't go to that door, you will still be in time, do not hurry ..." In effect, he understood that if he would resist, no one could force him to step over the threshold of this institution. But on the other hand, what kind of idiot would he look like? In fact, he could insist right at the beginning of "we apply for the license"—and there would be no more body movements. Had he behaved this way? No. He actually gave the agreement to marry now, without any delay. To run was cowardice and boyishness. Serge stood, similar to the beetle, not knowing what to undertake ...

Janna jumped out of the entrance. She was excited and solemn. Tall and athletic, she always moved easily and quickly, and in a second, she stood near Serge. Her hair was a little messy and her eyes burned. In them there was no hint of doubt: she decided to become a wife—in fact his, Serge's, wife. It was difficult to imagine that someone now could dissuade her from it. She was very beautiful in her aspiration to belong to the person standing next to her, a little tipsy, and bleary eyed from the expectation of the forthcoming action. The door opened, and an elderly, portly man invited the groom and the bride inside ...

In a long narrow room, there was another couple, likewise getting an 'underground' marriage. A woman in red sat at a green table, and offered them chairs opposite her. Her face was dissatisfied, as if she stood at the conveyor and stamped an approaching newly-married couple. This monotonous work rather bothered her.

Serge became very tired while he was waiting to have all the papers completed. From far away the tired voice resounded from the registrar of marriages. Serge raised his eyelids, and in front of him was laying Janna's passport. Looking at her picture he thought, "My God, how very young she looks at sixteen."[33] Serge tried to understand something, but he was called and asked to give his signature.

---

33 Soviets issued passports at age 16.

The woman got up, and with an official voice congratulated them. They left. Nothing changed outside, or in the world. But Serge and Janna now were in a different state. Serge turned, poked a finger into Janna's stomach and asked: "So, now are you my wife?" She answered, "Yes!" and hung on his neck. From the windows of the bunker curious eyes watched. Serge lifted her in his arms and carried her across the road.

In the house many people desired to kiss the newlyweds. Janna was running around the room, pointing at Serge and shouting at the top of her lungs, "Look, this is my husband!" Then they began to drink everything that was lying around, and when it became dark the guests started to leave. Janna and Serge took a taxi and left too. But not home: they went to a friend who had mercy on the young couple and gave them both a house and a marriage bed ...

There too, they could not avoid a large gathering. They made Janna a veil of napkins. They shouted "Gorko, gorko"[34] persistently and often. Janna and Serge kissed long, and crazily, so that their lips became red and out of shape.

About midnight, everyone departed, and Serge fell into bed. He had drunk too much and did not remember his first marriage night. At daybreak he woke up, gripped a pillow with his teeth and thought long about the turn of his destiny.

The same afternoon, he left Kishinev. It seemed to him that all this was a dream. But it was reality, the huge half-page marriage stamp on his passport weighed down his pocket.

***

---

34 Gorko—It's a Russian tradition to yell this word, which means bitter. The meaning is that life is bitter, and the newlyweds must kiss to make everything sweet.

He arrived in Moscow early in the morning. He entered the house, changed his clothes, and then glanced in his parents' room. They lay with open eyes and looked at the ceiling. "I got married," said Serge, but silence was his only answer. Hesitating, he silently left and locked the door to his room. Certainly, his parents' opinion was different from his own. First of all, they considered his behavior simply swinish in relation to them. They could not recognize this marriage as lawful. Everything was done "not like other people do." They rejected his bride, whom they never saw in their life—and now she was his wife? Their rejection was untenable. A lot of time would need to pass until somehow, everything would calm down.

Several days passed in silence: they clearly let him know just how insulted they were. But somehow, one evening they began a conversation. It continued over the next few days, heavy with splashes of emotions, the drinking of heart medication, tears, and other attributes of the sudden misfortune. There was a strong opinion that Janna had wrapped him around her finger and put a ring on his, taking advantage of his inexperience and even infantilism. What for? It was clear: to replace a Jewish surname, to achieve the coveted Moscow registration,[35] or whatever else could be on the mind of this woman. When Serge tried to say that they loved each other, his explanations were either ignored or met by sarcasm.

There were almost daily calls from Janna, where she said she could not live another day in separation. She was ready to throw everything away and to fly like mad to the aid of her husband. Serge, though, considered her arrival

35 Moscow registration—You had to be registered to live and work in cities like Moscow. You could only receive the registration for certain valid circumstances, like marriage. This process is similar to the US immigration process.

premature and extremely inappropriate during this inflamed time. He had, he explained, two examinations left for the autumn. It was necessary to pass these tests, to prepare for the exams—but Janna's voice was breaking up and she asked him to come just for the weekend ...

At last, she could not bear any more and arrived herself. The terrible conversations were now directed towards her. Serge was not needed any more: it was necessary to find out what this woman had in her head. His parents were locked with her in a room, and the discussions bordered on torture. Janna sobbed.

"Were you a virgin? What do you want from my son? How much do you make? How much does your mother make?" asked Serge's mother. More terrible conversations ensued. Janna ran out on the terrace to cry in private, which caused even greater hostility from Serge's non-supportive father.

During one such conversation, Serge opened the door, approached Janna and lowered himself before her on his knees. He took her hands in his and began to kiss her palms. He then embraced her head, nestled against her cheek, and whispered: "That's it ... that's it ... calm down. Now everything will be over." He turned to his parents, and in a quiet, but firm voice said: "You are all very dear to me, and I hope you are not indifferent towards me either. Understand: I love this woman. I want to be with her and I want all this hysteria stopped." He got up, and pulled Janna to his room ...

"Oh Lord! If it was only so!" he thought. "Lies, lies—I didn't do this!" He sat by himself on an ottoman, like a little mouse, and listened to the commotion created in the next room. She had flown 1,000 kilometers to rescue him, to rescue them in the name of what—Moscow registration?

Bosh! In the name of the preservation of love! And he had not made two steps, though he could easily reconcile both parties. How much could he have done later to save their love, their sincere feelings? In this life, it appears, you need to struggle, fight, and tear with your teeth those who intrude on the sanctity of love between two human beings.

Certainly, tearing his parents with his teeth did not follow. They understood human words, and gradually, their tone began to soften. Janna managed to reduce their negative attitude towards her.

Conversations, already quiet and logically weighed, began. "Where will you live? You have three more years of school. Spouses should live together, but here in our house it is simply impossible. You have a sister who should study too ..." and so on and so on. The romanticism of relationships was replaced by real everyday questions. When Janna was getting ready to fly home to talk to her mother, though, more pressure was applied.

Serge, Janna, and his mother went outside. "OK Serge, let's go," invited Janna.

"He will not take you to the airport," said his mother.

"He told me he will."

"I know him better than you. He will do as I say."

Serge stood dead in his tracks, silent. Janna left by herself.

***

Part 2

Overboard

The old man opened his eyes, and looked around. Everywhere, was the quiet dark blue sea. In the distance, about eight to ten kilometers, the big city glimmered. The strip of land running to the edge of the sea, departed from it, and was lost in a murky perspiration of air. The boat rocked on soft waves. The sun ran almost three quarters of the day's route. "Perhaps it is time to begin," the old man whispered, and picked up his bottle of whiskey. He made two big drinks and accurately screwed on the lid. From a bag he took out ham and cheese sandwiches, and slowly, enjoying the food began to chew.

"Ah, memory, memory!" he said to himself, rubbing his forehead. "In fact I do not remember how or when I came to the firm thought of divorce. Little drops of water can change the shape of a stone."

Once he went with his uncle on an electric train, and for a solid hour, in enough detail, his uncle convincingly proved that women grow old earlier, and lose their appeal. This by no means affects sexual life and men, being in the prime of life, seek carnal joys elsewhere, and the marriage collapses. You need to marry girls younger than yourself and mold them to you, so that everything is where it belongs.

Serge's uncle himself was unfortunate in his marriage. But he did not get divorced: he lived with this woman whose mind was not a tenth share of his own, but continued to live with her, often washing down his sufferings with vodka. Serge respected him, and therefore trusted in all this rubbish.

The old man finished one sandwich. He again took a sip of whiskey. He started the second.

In his memory, the mean scene emerged when Janna arrived again in Moscow in late autumn. But she stopped at a girlfriend's, in a dorm of the architectural institute. Serge plodded there with a portfolio with statements of the applications for Janna to agree to divorce. But Janna burned through them with a cigarette. She then said that she wished to make love to Serge, perhaps for the last time. And they loved each other, and then Janna declared that now she would have a child, and no divorce could happen. She took his things, and ran out from the room. He remained naked, humiliated, and suppressed.

What was it? Anger, that destiny turned out this way? The desire for revenge on this youth who has surrendered? Only Janna could know the answer. But this scene made it a disgusting business: his love that did not have time to become stronger in his heart, dissolved. This happened during the period, when this love had to be grown carefully, like a crystal in a test tube.

Serge sent the application for divorce to the Kishinev court—in place of the registration of marriage. He long looked forward to the answer. Only after a year did the summons come.

Everyday student life lulled his old feelings, and he arrived in Kishinev with an empty and cold heart.

They sat again in some uncomfortable, smeared green painted room. "Is it true, you want a divorce?" asked the judge. Serge nodded. "Yes," Janna said, with an absent look around the room. The judge prepared the papers for a long time. Serge looked at Janna. She was quiet and proudly sat on a bench, and to Serge it seemed that once again in the Registry Office everything was done precipitately, incorrectly. In fact the valid reasons for divorce were really not there. He liked this woman. He even admired her. But it was difficult for him to understand whether he loved her then. He recalled Janna's words then, on the Odessa train platform: "If you leave—we will never meet again." How wise Janna was, when she authentically knew that separation—was a tomb for love ...

"No! Don't do this!" Serge suddenly screamed. He jumped to his feet and made a step towards Janna. "Janna, Jannoska, my darling, I love you. It is all a lie. I do not want to get divorced. Let's get out of here." He lifted her up, and crazily began to kiss her face. She embraced him, and they quickly headed to the door ...

***

"Oooh, Oooh!" howled the old man. "Well why didn't I do this back then? Why did I sit? What was I waiting for, and what was I thinking? That life was only beginning and that there were so many chances ahead. That I would find better. And life—blink—flew by. Don't separate from your loved ones: just grow with your blood flowing through them... Did I sprout like that? Nope, I did not even try."

He bobbed on the waves, like an uncontrollable little craft. Here he would be taken at the end, in the middle of the sea. At the end ...

"Yes-yes, it is time to clear out," whispered the old man. He bent over to get a bottle of whiskey and he felt tears welling in his eyes. He placed his face in his hands and silently began to sob ...

***

Since October 24, 1974, the date of their divorce, five years had passed. During this time Serge finished the civil engineering institute, and worked for about a year in his department at the institute. His work consisted of driving waves in a laboratory pool, and studying their destructive force on construction in the high sea. It is impossible to say that this occupation was very pleasant to him. He performed the most complicated formulas, making calculations on the huge institute computer, for which you needed to sign up for your turn. There was a lot of dry paper work. He wanted to dive into life and have communication with people, instead of spending time with books spotted by mathematical calculations.

An opportunity appeared. Somehow in the café, he got acquainted with the executive director of the regional newspaper—he was a fervent and funny guy of 32 years. He told Serge that there was an opening in his department for a correspondent, and after a while Serge received his first editorial task. After a second, and a third, he was hired by the newspaper and began to adapt to journalistic work.

In two years he decided "to go to the people."[36] He also went to a Komsomol[37] for Outstanding Construction in Siberia. In each edition, he agreed that he would write about the glorious work of the Moscow building team where he went as one of its leaders. But he never had a chance to write. No work deeds were ever completed. They worked on the construction of the Surgut beer factory. And the whole group consisted of children and little girls who were not able to find work close to their homes. They came without specialties, and without desire to work, but with a greater desire to get drunk until they squealed like pigs. Not a night passed without a fight in some hall or in some room. They fought among themselves, then fought united—against the young people from the Kazakhstan group.

---

36 "To go to the people"—this is a phrase from Gorky. It means "go and make your own life, earn."

37 Komsomol—Young Communist League. The organization served as a highly mobile pool of labor and political activism.

Bruises were raised, blood flew, and teeth were knocked out. What body of communistic propaganda could publish articles about such a life? Serge could not lie and write cheerful material. At last, most of the violence was driven out, and many ran away from there. Life in the dorm calmed down and even achieved some civilized features. It formed a drama group, and Serge began to write and direct his own plays, reflecting everyday life on the "Outstanding Komsomol Construction" site. They started having parties with contests and dancing, and many started signing up for sports so that life began to get better, in comparison to the initial period ...

One day when Serge entered the dorm, the senior babysitter (oh God, what a position!), who distributed the mail, gave him a slip of paper saying that he would get a telephone call at nine o'clock that evening. In full confidence that the conversation had been ordered by his parents, Serge sat in a waiting room and waited for the call. But the voice that came over the telephone line turned him to stone. On other end of the wire was Janna. His Janna! No, she was not his anymore. For a long time, she was not his Janna! The conversation was about nothing. Serge learned that she married and had a daughter, Allochka.[38] She said she was doing well and had a husband in Kishinev, and asked how he was doing "in his poor Surgut". "What are you doing there fool? You are ruining your life? Do you think it is given to you forever?"

In response, Serge mooed something unintelligible. The stiffness did not go away. The allotted call time was over, and the quick beeps of a hang up were heard. "Even here she found me again," he thought. "She was not lazy: in fact, she needed to order a long distance call and eventually pay.

---

38 Allochka—term of endearment for the name Alla

What for? Almost six years after the divorce." Serge went down a footpath, creaking in his felt boots. Pines, branches weighed down with snow, looked as if they wished to share the grief that unexpectedly tore into his core. "She is not indifferent to me. Otherwise, why would she call? Out of sight, out of mind. Maybe she wanted to tease me. And here I am. I live without you and everything is all right with me, and you are freezing there in Siberia. Yes, the husband, the child ..." Something like a pain insultingly made its way to his chest and ruthlessly squeezed it.

"In fact, I married a girl in '76 too, in Kiev. I too, got acquainted with her on vacation on the sea, on the Caspian Sea. And then, we continued to live in different cities, and divorced easily without shouts and tears." Suddenly an idea came into his head that he never thought of before. Precisely. In fact Tanya, his second wife, very much resembled his first, Janna. She too was tall and long-legged, with long black hair. But she was without that vital spark which was, and in the course of time probably only, developed in Janna. "Certainly, I tried, obviously not realizing, to find a copy of Janna. To revive Janna, but in another person. The attempt did not go right, because another woman like Janna does not exist in this world."

"Fool!" is an inherently insulting word, but when she said it somehow softly with some kind of vexation the word found material embodiment and grew in meaning. "What have you done for the past six years?" he asked himself. "What have you achieved? You already lost two wives. You remain without children. What do you have, except for these felt boots and a short fur coat? With whom do you communicate? With boys and little girls who never held books in their hands? Who have you surrounded yourself with here? What do you wish to fish out from this?"

With such cheerless ideas, Serge returned to the dorm and fell on the creaking cot.

It is quite probable that this call was a catalyst. Serge began to gather his things and soon returned to his publisher ...

***

Some more years passed. Serge got up to his ears in the business of constructing youth-inhabited complexes—it was lively work during the musty years of the early 80s. Janna let him know about herself again. He found out that she divorced, but she did not dwell on the details or the reasons, at least with him. Anyway, she was free again. Serge was also free, and in the summer of '84 both of them vacationed in Crimea. They were absolutely close to each other: she was in Koktebel, and Serge was near Sudak. She called him to come, but he did not move in her direction.

***

"Well why, why, why?" the old man moved his lips, unscrewing the top from the bottle. "What or who stopped you? That passion from which you were then on vacation? But in fact, you left her as soon as you arrived in the Moscow station. Did you believe that it is impossible to glue together a broken vessel? Or, were you stopped by the fact that this woman already had a child? No. All these reasons are nonsense. You have not moved from your spot due to your laziness, and you could not recognize where your happiness is. And it was next to you, just a few kilometers away. You could have met, and the warm sea, the hot sun would revive old feelings. In fact you remember the good.

The bad is forgotten. How to know, in any case, that back then, it was not too late ..."

The old man inserted the neck of the bottle into his mouth and greedily drank the bitter liquid. He frowned and rinsed an apple in the seawater ...

***

Several more months passed. Serge received a letter:

My daughter has a warm nose. She is like from an animated cartoon. This person is the purpose of my life. She sits down at the piano, and plays and sings a simple song. I am happy.

And when I distract myself from haste and hurry, I notice sometimes the blue sky, the sun, and it becomes sad. Why? Is it necessary to explain it on paper? I wrote you in my thoughts, many letters, but on paper they would seem so banal. And here is this one. Shall I send it in 1973 or in now? And what if someone laughs about it, and what if it seems ridiculous or sentimental?

Your eyes appear unexpectedly; they appear from there, from '73, they appear with sea drops on eyelashes ... Everywhere: on the face of a clock, in a trolley bus, on a beach, in a hurry. I talk to you, but I speak, and for the answer, I do not wait. Then I banished you to an eleven-year distance, but not for long. How have you lived all this time, then? What didn't you love, and what did you love? It seems to me, I know the answers to these questions. Somehow, you said that it is necessary to wait for two years. I agreed and I waited eleven years. And for what? Simply, for a conversation with you. Maybe you are the one, with whom it is possible to conclude a phase of life—in fact these 11 years are a whole eternity. All of us are afraid of banalities, but in fact life consists of them. And the clean bed and the tasty meal is not everything that is necessary for a two-legged. And the fact that from our gorgeous head fall curls of gold, is just that firstly, you have not seen me for a long time, and secondly, that our globe spins, and we are spinning together with it, and moreover, we try to overtake its rotation with personal and public transportation and we do this so diligently—that some add one year—and others immediately add eleven.

I am torn by a desire to meet; that is why I play out different possibilities. Do you wish to take part in this game?

It seems to me that our meeting would not be a return to the ashes. Can you understand all this in the Moscow vanity?

I was glad to write to you, remaining with the surname of my first husband.

Janna

***

Yes they met. But both were late. Serge had already married a third time, and with his wife, waited for the birth of a child. He did not tell Janna this.

Janna was more than beautiful. The years did not show on her. She was graceful, but she was already a mature woman, lush and stunning. Serge looked at her and understood that in the Moscow hurry he wasted eleven years when he could have lived them with this smart and strong woman. And to live them absolutely differently and for sure his life would be full, and he would be more joyful than he was all these past years. But now, he entered the next phase of his stay on this ground, and he was already keen for the creation of a new family in which he already would have children.

They sat in his sister's apartment, and they gradually talked about everything. However, Serge tried to imagine the opportunity of a reunion ... What has climbed into his inflamed head? That the child won't be born or that he would leave his wife with the child? Timidity and cowardice— they caused this delirium. He sat on the sofa, and his heart was broken from regret that they lived different lives, instead of one joined. And the reason for it was only his cowardice. He, now as a man, was attracted to this woman. He wouldn't mind recalling once more the warmth of her body and then leaving, perhaps forever. But at this time she appeared more strong than he, and overcame in herself the desire for closeness. Although, who's to say, maybe she did not want it anymore. This meeting seemed so sad—like from an orchestra pit, sounded the coda.

But life ordered that many years later they would hear from each other again.

***

The Soviet Union collapsed into the many pieces that were its components. Republics became separate states. Moldavia became Moldova, and represented something distant and almost inaccessible. Somewhere there was Janna, and Serge remained in Russia, which was pulled as with a vacuum cleaner, into the days that were extremely vague. Both above and below,[39] clearly no one knew what to do. They needed to develop market relationships, or in other words to revive capitalism. It seemed to many, that having thrown off communistic fetters, life would immediately improve, would develop the creativity of the masses and cause the sun to blossom above the country once again. But the reality was far from this vision. Almost all branches of the national economy began to decay and wither. Business life almost stopped. The budgetary sphere received a deep crack. People had no money, yet strangely they wished to eat, drink, equip their dwellings, travel, and in general have

39 Above and below—refers to the government and the people.

everything that enters into the concept of a full-blooded life. And people, on any step of the hierarchical ladder that they found themselves on during this muddy time, began to reach for this full-blooded life independently, as their own conscience allowed. It was like sharing a vast pie, which was previously called the material and financial base of the great country. But rules on how to divide it did not exist. Under the law of the jungle, tidbits go to the strongest. Gangster factions bred like mushrooms. They were at war among themselves and with the authorities, although the authorities were not strong enough to oppose them. Racketeering prospered. Everyone who tried somewhere, somehow to earn money, had to pay a tribute irrespective of whether you stood in a bazaar and you traded, or you sold, or you tried to be involved in private enterprise or commerce.

Strangely enough, in this initial period Serge was fortunate. He became occupied with the then-popular tourism that placed foreign guests with families. There came mostly Germans, English, and Americans, to gape at this strange country that had been closed by the Iron Curtain. Foreigners paid several tens of dollars for accommodation with families—for them a trifle, but for us, huge money. They drove around Moscow by taxi, paying with packs of *Marlboros*—and everyone was happy. Serge was happy too. His family did not starve. And he managed to carry his wife and then still small children "on excursion" to Hungary (which also at that time shed its communistic skin), and to visit almost all the countries of Europe, and even to go to America.

But one day Serge thought that he could earn more with construction, since he was a certified and registered engineer, and he opened his own business. Once again, he forgot that from the good you do not search for better. But he made this step, and it subsequently led to his best years of blossoming, spent in the continuous struggle against debt and poverty ...

The beginning, though, did not foretell anything bad. Orders were coming in. The firm grew. Serge equipped his office and sat there at the head of a long table. Everything was as it needed to be: a secretary, an accounting department, a marketing department, a supply group, and working brigades. And during this period, somehow a phone rang. It was Janna. She zeroed in on him again, though she called from the USA where she had recently moved for permanent residence. Outside it was 1992. Janna suggested that he trade with America, and sent a list of prices on foodstuffs. In fact, hungry Russia needed to eat something. But why should he engage in a business unusual for his firm, when his business was booming? The contact faded, but the shining skin on Serge's face was barely wrinkled from the surging memories. "Well," he thought, "why is she not here, next to me, or why am not there? In fact, together we could move mountains. She has a bloodhound's nose to sniff out the direction of where and what you need to move. This is how ... she moved to America, taking with her both her daughter and her mother! Amazing!"

"And you, as a matter of fact, are alone. You have assistants that will run away in a moment if something scares them. You sit, and become snobby. But for certain, something is not right; you make mistakes and you do not notice ..."

The mistakes did not take long to be shown. The whole year of 1993, the dollar *stood* as dead: prices grew, but the rate of the dollar was constant. Everyone who was engaged in import grew rich, by leaps and bounds. Everybody bought the goods for one thousand dollars. They sold for rubles under the increasing prices. They exchanged rubles at a cheap and stable rate. They were selling it to their seller, not forgetting to leave, "some extra money" overseas, or here, in Russia. Serge lamented his shortsightedness. "What did you reject? Janna was offering you, this very thing, as if she could predict favorable market conditions. But you had agreements based on the dollar. It was good for the customer—you bring them dollars, you change them for a cheap rate, and then run to the market to buy materials that are rising in price every day. That's all. It's done. Failure is waiting for you. When Janna offered prosperity ... she again stretched her hand out to you. She herself was in serious need of money. Aren't these preconditions for a strong alliance? Well big deal, she is your former wife. That's even better. It is not necessary to explain to each other who you are." But Serge missed this chance, by his own foolishness and because of his own conceit.

"Trouble has come—open the gate." And literally, on the threshold of his office gangsters appeared ...

It was July 9, 1993. And on July 8th Serge in the circle of his whole family, celebrated his mother's 65th birthday. He was still a little tipsy when he arrived at his office. He got out of the car, and was immediately surrounded by enforcers. Yes, they were gangster drones. They ransacked the city in search of rich dealers who were not yet "protected." (Almost all the businessmen already had a "roof" or gangster, either bandits or FSB.[40] These "protectors" included former Afghan soldiers, and sportsmen, and my god, everybody was in ...)

They did not introduce themselves. They said that they would arrive tomorrow for conversation, because now they didn't have time. They offered friendship and

---

40 Russian Federal Security Service—former KGB

services: shaking off debtors, resolving problems with pig-headed customers—in short, they had the kindest of intentions. "And as a token of friendship," they said, "Give us cigarettes." And Serge gave. How could he have known, being raised in an intelligent family, that in gangster rules this step was referred to as the purchase of "the right of the first night?" You have given money; it is unimportant how much. You have given, so you have invited them to visit you. You have subscribed under the certificate of "cooperation." Nobody else, according to the thieves' rules, could do anything more to this client—he was already under a roof.

The next day they came as promised, at eleven in the morning. One of them muscular like a bull with a shaved nape, strode through the office master-like and, asking nobody, opened Serge's door. Silently, with a nod of his head he invited Serge to get out—we will talk in the car. He opened the back door of the car; two men—the driver and one more shaved head, sat in the front seat. The one, who invited Serge, sat next to him in the back seat. Later, Serge learned that to sit down in the car under any circumstances was dangerous. But could he allow himself to look like a coward?

There was no preamble. Serge immediately felt the impact of a sideways fist. In truth, he was not beaten strongly; he was beaten just for the sake of intimidation.

"You will pay us. Do you hear? Do you understand?" said the guy who was sitting in the front, not even turning around. "You make big money here, so ten grand a month for you is not a stretch. I do not hear your answer!"

Again, there was a blow in his side. But Serge was ready for it and clenched his muscles. The impact was weaker than the first.

"Well! Why are you silent? Who do you take us for, you fuck! You think it is OK to play silent with us?"

"So go to the forest, he will tell us something faster," said the driver, impatiently starting the ignition.

"No need to go to the forest," Serge said calmly. He didn't know why, but he didn't have any fear.

Later, by himself in his office, he shook like an aspen leaf, and the young secretary offered to call an ambulance. But now, he was externally unperturbed. He got a cigarette from his pocket and lit it.

"Ten thousand dollars a month—the sum is unreal. You have incorrect information on my business. If you want, we will go, and you can check my accounts."

Serge understood that now, these morons will not go anywhere because they understand crap about accounting. He needed to delay a little bit, and his brain convulsively thought how to get out of this tin box. "Scream, or call for help?" he thought to himself. Next to them was a little park, where only moms with children walked by.

"You will get a punch in your jaw and then they certainly drive you away. Jump out and run to the office. You can always find some hefty guys in the supply department ... I will make noise, and what then? The bandits will guard the building until night. It is impossible to jump out so quickly: the door is locked, you need to pull up the lock button, you have to open the door ... I need to win them over, somehow calm them down."

"Don't give us shit. We know everything. We already checked everything. In short, ten grand, on the 30th of each month. And don't get the thought in your head to run to the police or somewhere else. We will find you. So, I don't hear the answer!"

"Ah," he realized, "They need an answer; this is what they need. They want me to give them a promise. I'll give one—then the shit hits the fan ... "

"I will talk about the sum and the rest of the terms with your boss. Tomorrow or during any time convenient for him, I am ready to meet. And now, please excuse me, I have a customer coming, and if I'm not there, there will not be ten, or five, or even three grand." Serge spoke so easily and convincingly that the thought of a lie or dirty trick didn't even cross their minds.

"Well, shall we believe this asshole? Tomorrow, also at eleven, we will take you where it's needed, you'll talk ... Don't get it into your head to run from us. We know where to find you."

Serge opened the door, slowly got out of the car, and slowly moved towards his office. He had only a day to find a way to rescue himself, his family, and maybe his business. Though he didn't really believe that he could rescue his business ...

After two years of persistent struggle, he sold a four-bedroom house in Moscow and took his family abroad. But this gave him only relative serenity. Earning money was extremely difficult. Although sometimes he was lucky, his good fortune was coming to an end, and poverty was coming, pitiful and humiliating. Serge did not notice how he grew older and completely exhausted. He could not do anything positive any more—his knowledge, and his steel experience, was not in demand ...

***

"One needs to die in his mother land," the old man whispered, putting his legs on a stone. Back on the beach, he tied the stone with strong hempen ropes. Now he needed to attach his feet to these ropes. For this purpose, he chose a thin nylon twine that was easier to push under the hemp. The sun was rapidly setting. He needed the light of the slanting beams to handle this work, and not to do it by touch. He passed the twine under the hemp, then wound the end around his right ankle, stretched the cord, and again passed it under the rope. He did this until he tied it around his leg thirteen times. He chose the number thirteen because this number appeared in his life many times, and for him, it was lucky. It is difficult to explain why he decided to make it so. He was neither a superstitious nor a devout person. He simply decided to do so—that's it. When the right leg was firmly attached, he started on the left. This business went more quickly because he already gained some experience. About ten minutes later, the left leg was attached to the stone. He fastened the end with a sea knot. The rest of the cord he cut off and threw out into the sea. His legs with veins that were dark blue even before entanglement, began to become even bluer. The blood supply had obviously worsened.

"That's OK," the old man calmed himself. "There is not that much left."

The crimson sun went down to the edge of the sea. He observed the beauty of a sunset many times. But here, far from the beach, the sunset was especially impressive. It seemed that the fiery sphere was just about to touch the water and the violence of the elements would begin. It seemed the sea would begin to boil and start to extinguish the heavenly body. He even imagined that clouds of steam would rise in the sky, and looked at how fast the space becomes thinner between the bulk of the sun and the far away strip at the end of the horizon. The red rays were still trying to sink their teeth into the sea, but they reflected on the surface and left slanting lines in the sky. A bright path ran from his boat straight to the falling disk flaring from its last efforts. Black glasses allowed him to look at this miracle of nature without serious consequences. The old man began to count—two more minutes and the sun will begin to fade, somewhere there, far in the boundless waters. As soon as the sun touched the water then he, the old man, would follow it. So he envisioned. This was his plan. His algorithm of actions.

Really, he did not have time to count to a hundred. As the sun reached the horizon, the sea looked as though it began to eat the fiery sphere.

"Well that's it, it's time," the old man said in a half-voice. He pulled out a battery-powered drill from a sack. He tested it and thrust the drill, like a corkscrew, into the wooden bottom of the boat. The drill went softly, without effort, piercing the wet boards. The old man was surprised at the speed. Suddenly the drill, not meeting any obstacle, plunged down to the drill-bit housing. The old man pulled out the drill. From the hole, a fountain of water cheerfully sprang up.

"It is possible to drill more, and the process will be accelerated," the old man thought. But the spurting ran so vigorously that the need for an additional hole disappeared. The old man examined the drill—excellent German work— then swung and threw it far from the boat.

The water was coming. When the boat loses buoyancy, it will quickly sink, and the heavy stone (the old man had barely dragged it in the boat) would drag him to the depths. What depth, the old man did not know. Perhaps a hundred-two hundred meters. He removed his glasses and looked inside the sea, but except for darkness, he didn't see anything. Only waiting remained.

The sun disappeared as if it was a piece of butter in a heated frying pan. Water already filled the bottom of the boat.

"No one will search for me," the old man reflected. "If they do, it will be short. Nobody will search the bottom of the sea for some mad man. And thank God. There will be none of those nervous and expensive preparations for a funeral, there will be no foolish speeches at a tomb, there will be no ridiculous commemoration when after half an hour of toasts for resting in peace everyone starts to crack about everyday ordinary affairs: how many seeds you need to plant in the garden of a dacha and when to expect blooms... No, I will fence myself and my relatives from this vulgarity. So this is how I want it, how I ordered it in my will!"

The boat was a quarter full; the stone and everything was in water. The sun disappeared, the sea swallowed it. The dark blue of the sky became lead, and this lead outflow covered the sea from the opposite side where the sun left.

The old man closed his eyes and began to whisper the lines written long ago:

You do not trust me—I'll forgive
To be angry, I'll never learn.
I have only one thing to ask you:
Allow me to quench my thirst from your gentle lips.

Yes, I have escaped to the country of charming dreams,
Let the rusting leaves cover the ground,
Let the disgusting wind blow between birches,
Dejectedly, they lower along their bodies their palms.

Let the rain of grief wash the heart of sadness,
And heat the soul ruthlessly.
It was everything—in spite of this, someone is missing
Someone is missing last night, and now.

I am forgotten ... Everything failed as if in eternity,
And maybe, were carried away in transcendental cold.
I remained alone. Around—my carelessness
Glasses ring. Can you hear? 'Ding'!

It is so silent, so melodious ...
Crystal, and maybe, Czech glass.
I hear a whisper: "Darling, do you love me?"
Oh my God! Who has this thick glass tumbler?

Chuckles, coming nearer,
And a hoarse voice nasally mumbling:
"I smelled it, oh really—they are pouring.
Give me a shot—my insides burn."

But who are you, with a blue nose
The dribbling mouth, a shivering lip
Sickly chest, belly pump (the stomach sucks everything)
Where are you thrusting your hand?

Get away! Image, disappear,
Your face is impossible to me.
Have mercy, for this delusion—
It seems your features are familiar to me.

Well, good for you, you noticed our similarity,
But I thought everything was bad for me.
But you are ingenious, and through the ugliness
To recognize the corpse—in fact it is me!

I walk after you as a shadow.
I follow you, without rest.
Either night you will live through, or day,
And I still wait for you ...

And with each hour faster and faster
 You slide into my embrace.
 You the sinner! You fell victim of passions,
 But that's OK, repent in my monastic cell.

The jaw froze in mid-scream,
But the desert gobbled up the wild cry.
Around all shadows prowl, patches of light,
Oppressive anguish falls on the chest.

A salty tear washes my soul,
Cold sweat irrigated the bed.
I know, just simply I'm missing someone
And last night, and now.

You do not trust me—I'll forgive,
I'll never learn anger, not at all.
I only have one thing to ask you:
Allow me to quench my thirst from your lips.

Yes, I have escaped to the country of a dream,
And in it I catch up with you,
I love you from here, believe me!
Whether I can love you in reality,
I do not know at all.

***

The old man wiped the tears running on his cheeks, and with pleasure remembered the bottle. "Yes," he continued, taking a large drink. "They will gather anyway. Anyway, in any case, they will eulogize me regardless of the letter which I left in the hotel to be read by my family. Family? But which one? During your life in this world, you, brother, created a heap of families. But you weren't the real head, the provider in any of them ... So, you were the lover, and the physiological father. You were a pain and a splinter. The ruiner of souls you were. And how many hearts have you shattered? How many gentle maiden hearts have you crushed with indifference, arrogance, and emptiness? And in spite of this fact, you violently fell in love, losing your head, and during these moments you could take your last shirt and give it to whom you loved. But as soon as passion cooled, the loved one ceased to exist ... Everyone suffered, but you also suffered from all of this confusion and disorder. Where is this coming from, from whom, from what ancestor?"

Water began to wash the soles of his feet. The old man wished to lift them, but in making the effort he remembered that he was attached. His already intoxicated brain reminded him why he, in general, was here. He dangled in the middle of the blackening sea. Ah, yes. Now everything will become black. And, at last, the ordeals in this life will be over.

Despite the tragedy of the situation, the old man was absolutely calm. His pulse was strong and rhythmical, barely faster. But it was more likely from the drink, rather than the sensation of his nearing end.

"But, in fact my mind can leave me, when it begins. In fact I can start panicking. And I would want to leave with dignity. Although nobody sees me ... But even so, for myself. In fact, how cold-bloodedly Martin Eden[41] left. And Bunin's Mitia, who with force and pleasure, shot himself in his mouth. And old man Hem? Oh, Janna, precious Janna. You wanted me to like this writer! Yes I liked him. I read everything of his. And I know that he left by will. And I, the old man, dangle now in a half-sunk boat. But I do not struggle with a huge fish, and I am simply waiting for when my body will go to these fishes to be eaten up."

"My kind and gentle Janna! Forgive that I ran from you my whole life and searched for those who even externally resembled you—in this paradox of my whole private life. How silly and ridiculous this is! To know for my entire life, that there actually lives in the world the dearest person, and I disappeared and hid for my entire life from my own happiness, artificially dulling the feelings for a while, feelings of love for the girl from 1973—the most miraculous year of my life. But now everything will end. The absurd should have a logical ending. Perhaps it is silly to die, but it is more silly to continue this futile existence. Everything is lost, everything is already behind. Now the fish and the sea worms will begin their business ..."

Here the old man winced. He imagined a skeleton standing on the stone, which as the diligent carrier of food delivered it to the bottom of the sea. The mouths of tiny fish poked at the skeleton that was presented to them, biting off tasty morsels. And this skeleton would be him, himself. "Now you are sitting and philosophizing, sipping whiskey, and tomorrow when the sun creeps out of the water again, you will not creep out any more—you will remain there, in darkness forever. Forever!" This word forced him to shudder again. But he immediately took control of himself. "It is enough to become limp! You were preparing for this for a long time. Isn't it all the same to you, which barracuda

---

41 Martin Eden—main hero in Jack London's novel of the same name. He commits suicide by drowning.

will peck you? A couple of minutes of cramps—and I spit on everything... So the business will not go like this! Now you will start to untie yourself." And so that there was no temptation, the old man threw overboard the diving knife which had not left his side since the time he trained as a diver.

The sides of the boat lowered right to the surface of the water. Smooth waves did not flow inside yet, but the moment was already close. As soon as sea water rushed through the board it would be too late to count the minutes. The old man already sat on his calves in the water. His feet were cold, though from alcohol his body was warm and did not freeze. Stars in harmony lit up in the sky, but everywhere you looked, the ominous blackness of the rapidly-approaching southern night gaped. It was lighter only on the side where the lights of the big city went up into the sky.

The old man shook the bottle—there was still a good quarter of un-sipped liquid. But he did not want to sip it. But he also did not want the good liquor to be lost. The old man tightly closed the cork and let the bottle swim. Then he put his elbows on his knees and lowered his head to his palms. For some time he lost consciousness. Many pictures from his own life flashed in front of his eyes, grinning, he could not understand in any way with what speed his thought penetrated the depths of the lived years. Suddenly in front of his eyes built up a line of his close and distant relatives, those living now and those who had already passed. But the memory resurrected the dead. All of them were strenuously peering at him: grandfathers and grandmothers, aunts and uncles, parents, sisters, and his own children. One grandmother was crossing herself; another was whispering something with flattened by time lips. One grandfather shook his fist; the other nervously smoked. The parents were standing pale; the kids were crying. On all their faces he could read one question: To whom will he join now? To those who are alive or dead? "They love me ..." As if in a delirium, the old man spoke, and suddenly straightened himself up. "In fact they all love me!" he shouted out, and at the same moment a stream of tears sprung from his eyes. "And do I love all of them? What am I doing? Going away! I am running away from a life on the earth to those who are already underground. No, I am running away from them as well. In fact I am hiding under the water. I duped everyone one time more. Ha-ha-ha!" The old man's harrowing laugh scattered above the sea. Suddenly a feeling of the deepest tenderness toward all the people he'd ever met flowed through his whole body, and he whispered: "Forgive me! Forgive me and for this I cannot get out of here ..."

Suddenly, the old man felt that someone else was in the boat. This someone was his own corpse. "Oh, here we meet at last," breathed the old man as he started shivering. It became scary to him; he had never experienced anything like it. A horror stole into him: he clearly saw death.

A splash was heard. It was a wave that went over the top of the gunwales, and the boat immediately became heavier. "Two more such waves and everything will be over." The old man spoke in catalepsy, and his hand convulsively stretched out to the ropes. But they had became wet and did not want to be untied. Besides, to unwind them, time was needed. There wasn't any more time left. The old man began to take out handfuls of water: the instinctive animal actions of a dying person. "The ropes should be cut. But with what? I threw out everything." Panic possessed him, although he understood that panicking was not allowed.

But there was no decision. A chance for rescue did not remain. There was only a sinking boat, a stone, and himself, fatally tied to this stone. No drill, no knife—he even threw out the bottle. Stop! He did not throw out the bottle. He simply launched it near the boat. A hope shone. "Oh, how those who are drowning grasp at straws!" The old man began to drive his hands behind the board, trying to find this hell-bound bottle. But only warm water stroked his palm. And suddenly: a miracle! He heard a quiet knock of something firm against the boards of the boat. The knock was coming from somewhere near the bow of the boat, where he sat on the bench. Slowly, so as not to overturn the little craft, he began to reach with his whole length, to reach this object. There was his bottle of whiskey—he did not have any doubts. He lay down with his chest on the front bench. It seemed to him that he had to scoot Janna over. The delusion was not going away.

"Where has the bottle gone?" It swam away, probably. His legs were pulled together in pain. Maybe the knock was imaginary? He lowered his hand and with his fingers found the glass. Yes it was his bottle that did not want to leave at all, like a piece of a spaceship that floated nearby. He splashed with his palm, like a flipper, and the bottle neck appeared between his fingers. The old man cautiously lifted his hand and dragged the bottle into the boat, and looked at the bottle as if sure rescue came with it. No, it was just giving him a weak chance. Mainly, it brought some goal orientation into the actions of the old man.

He crawled back and tried to reach the ropes. He managed this. The boat by some miracle was holding on the surface, but was ready to sink at any moment.

The old man swung and knocked the bottle on the boards of the boat. It shattered, but in his hand remained the neck with sharp edges. He dove under and groped for the rope which was tied to the stone, and began to cut it. The rope, it seemed, was not impressed. In fury, the old man began to gnash the glass on the stone, assuming that he was sawing the rope. But when he again tried to find a cut, he found nothing. The top boards on the boat were barely 10 centimeters above the water. Very soon it would be completely filled with water—and then everything that was still holding on the surface would slowly and uncontrollably fall into the abyss. The old man became terrified again. He was overcome with a nervous shivering. But he managed to take himself in hand and began to repeat one calming phrase: "Don't panic! Only don't panic ..."

Bending over, he seized in a death grip the shackles that he so recently carefully fastened. He loosened a bit of rope from the stone to wedge in a shard of glass, and began to drive it quickly back and forth, like a hacksaw. He did not watch the list of the boat, not allowing himself any distraction, and concentrated only on his work. At last the strings of hemp were cut off. Now he needed to pull out the end of the rope that was reeled around his legs. But the rope was so tightly tied that he immediately abandoned this attempt. He either needed to cut the rope in three places because the stone was tied up like a cross, or to cut the many nylon ropes that encircled his legs. Neither that nor anything else in this situation could save him—he was too pressed for time. "This means that what I conceived will nevertheless come to pass. But while the boat is still floating, I cannot stop. And then, it will be what it will be. In five or ten minutes everything will be over—several convulsive movements, and everything will dim. And then everything becomes absolutely indifferent. But while it has not yet happened, I need to cut."

The old man pulled one string of the hempen rope and cut it easily, like with a sharp knife. But there were many loops, and though he managed to finish the remaining coils more easily, insidious time ran more quickly. Then he began to cut the ropes directly on his leg, sticking the sharp glass into his skin. He almost didn't feel the pain. He only understood that the wound became larger and larger. "As long as I don't cut a vein," the old man thought. And suddenly one leg was easily released. He even screamed in gladness. But the other remained tethered. He looked at the boards of the boat and was surprised: they floated under water. The nose was sticking out, and in the stern the old man sat up to his waist in water. But the boat was not sinking. Why? He could not find an explanation. "Goodness, this sea monster supports me regardless." But he needed to unravel himself instead of this riddle. He undertook the second leg.

"So, if I am holding on the top of water, we shall try to manage without trauma. If I cut holes in myself, it is all the same in the end. Blood in sea water will not cease flowing." The old man felt like a skilled surgeon, when he began to accurately cut thread after thread on the ropes on his left leg. Already half were gone; here remained only few more waves of his glass weapon ...

Unexpectedly, something with noise jumped out behind his back, and the stern promptly began to plunge. The old man impulsively threw his body overboard the sinking little craft. But the leg, which was carried away by a monstrous force, pulled him downwards. He waved his hands to fill his lungs with air. He immediately came across something firm. It was a cork life jacket. "So this is why the boat was sinking so slowly," he realized. "It lay under the stern and I did not notice it." The old man seized this pitiful float and thus remained on the surface. The boat stood almost vertically. In its nose there was still air, but it left singing through thin cracks. The stone became stuck under a bench. Now this vessel will go to the bottom. And all its mass will drag him down, so no life jacket will help. And would the life vest sustain him together with the stone? But for this experiment, he knew, he must as a minimum, take the stone out of the boat. To dive and pull out—in fact it was easy; the stone in water had lost its initial weight. Yes, to pull out the stone was possible, but in doing so he would not emerge any more. In fact, he needed to let the life vest go.

These thoughts crossed his brain like lightning while he convulsively tried to pull the life vest onto himself. One hand managed to pass into the half sleeve, but it was impossible for the second to catch the opening. He began to jerk his leg, trying to pull it from captivity. But these attempts were in vain. "My God, what a fool I am. In fact I only need to unwind only three or four threads of this rope ... I'm wasting time in vain. While the boat stays here, it means I need to dive and unwind." The old man looked at the nose of the boat sticking out in the darkness, took some deep breaths and exhalations, breathed in air and slipped out of the life vest. He drew in his foot and, with difficulty, carefully forced himself not to make sharp movements, as he began to pull the rope. He successfully loosened one thread, and undertook the second. It was pulled out quickly ... But what was this? His ears began to squeeze. The old man mechanically pinched his nose and blew, but the pressure in his ears kept building.

He felt the movement of water around him. He understood that the boat had gone under water and pulled him into a chasm. He clamped his nose with one hand and again began to blow out through it, leveling the pressure in his ears. With the other hand he pulled the remaining two strings. One of them would not give in. Then he took up the other—and it quickly slipped off, and then the rest of the rope crawled off too. The old man felt his stomach being pushed under his ribs, and felt the first pangs of suffocating waves run through his body. He made a stroke with his arms, but knew that he had lost his orientation. The leg was at last liberated, but it was not clear which way was the surface or the bottom. He was surrounded by utter darkness. The old man lifted his hand to his mouth, let out a bubble of air, and only the bubbles showed him the way. It appeared that he had somehow swum diagonally deeper, but he instantly changed direction and chased after the bubbles. Attacks of asphyxiation accrued. If only he could hold his breath, and not exhale—otherwise with the next breath, water would pour into him. The old man kicked his legs like a frog, and began greater and stronger strokes with his hands.

But the long-awaited surface was too far away. "Where has it dragged me—fifteen meters down, or more? To such a depth I didn't dare dive, even as a youth with flippers ..." The feelings of asphyxiation suddenly stopped, and he knew the next step: oxygen starvation and loss of consciousness. And still—he knew he couldn't exhale, but had to keep going incrementally upwards, without hurry, without panic ... It seemed to him, that he was stroking for an eternity, that he already turned into a fish and lived there, in the depths of the sea. Suddenly his hand plunged into something jellylike. With loathing, he tried to swim away from the big jellyfish, but the tentacles nevertheless hooked on him and painfully burnt him. Circles appeared in front of his eyes. They were either going farther, or coming nearer, and they were some strange, dark brown color. "Everything will now become dim," he thought. "The brain will be disconnected ..."

Already isolated and absolutely fearless, the old man thought hard. His sensations weakened, he easily and resignedly gave in to the charge of death, but still continued to stroke away from this monstrous abyss. His movements were slowed down, and no more strength remained in his muscles. So, haggard with pursed lips, he suddenly appeared on the surface. He took a breath, but not immediately, which is what usually happens. He lay on his back and let out the burnt air, then greedily took a gulp of fresh air. He floated and breathed often, restoring his breath, and watched with interest as life returned to him. Gradually the circles disappeared. He began to distinguish stars in the sky. The light sway of the water lulled him, and he stayed on his back, as though the business was done and there was no need to swim any longer. Indeed, he had no desire to swim anywhere, but felt like lying back and enjoying his second birth. But it would be more correct to say, returning from that other world, the world of the dead.

He felt a shiver. He literally shook from the cold, as if something was vibrating somewhere inside him. His teeth knocked against each other. He moved to a vertical position. He began to look around, but except for the sea dissolved in darkness, he saw nothing. He remembered that he wounded himself and that blood certainly poured from him. He grasped his anklebone, and then brought his hand directly to his eyes and saw that even the water did not have time to wash off the black as ink blood in the darkness. He removed his swimming trunks. With difficulty he ripped them and tightly tied up his leg. How long could he swim this way? This was not known to him.

But to swim was necessary. Where? Where was the nearest coast? He pivoted around and saw nothing. But then, he saw only the glow of the big city in the distance. But there was no point trying to swim there—it was too far. The coast, though also invisible, was closer on the left side of the glow. He needed to swim about five or six kilometers, guessing the direction, in utter darkness.

Having made a few strokes, he understood that he had obviously lost his way and was swimming in circles. He lay on his back and tried to orient himself by the stars. Besides the Big Dipper, he knew little. But his luck was obviously drawn in the dark sky. Here, is the Polaris star; directly above the dipper. Peering at it, and then looking lop-sided at the glow, he at last chose a way and swam on his back, trying not to deviate from the planned direction. He swam for a long time, but everything in the sky remained the same. What distance had he covered, and was it in the right direction? He turned over and started the breast stroke.

Once in a while, he turned around and looked for the saving star. His teeth were clenched from the cold. This hindered his breathing. He tried to swim more quickly to warm up, but became exhausted and switched to a more economical style. All the same, the fatigue was taking him over. He now had to rest for a long time, lying on his back. He almost did not feel his tied up leg. Gradually consciousness was leaving him. He moved like a robot only because it was necessary to move.

How much time passed—an hour, two, three, maybe more—he did not know. But when, heaven knows, will dawn come? This foolish night can't last eternally. But the dawn was not coming. He wanted to lie down in a hot bath. And he wanted to drink, a lot and long. The salty water, which he swallowed quite a lot, made him nauseous. "It is strange," he thought. "The water is all around me, but I could die of thirst." He turned over on his stomach and swam, trying to keep his movements rhythmical and his breaths even. So he swam, long and frenzied, seeing almost nothing in front of him. But here again he swallowed sea water. He cleared his throat. He swam some more and after a while again swallowed a big portion. He floated on his back and froze without movement, coming to his senses. He started to understand that he could not cope with this sea. It, evidently, would not release him. Then he would die, and that is what he came there for. It will happen, but not as he planned. But what is the difference? His arms did not move anymore; his leg had become stiff. Soon the waves would start to cover him, and everything would be over. So he reflected, calmly expecting the end. There was no desire to remember anything. The years lived did not pass before his eyes; he simply faded away, having spent all his vital forces.

Suddenly it seemed to him that the sky brightened. He turned back and saw a thin strip of dawn on the edge of the sea. Encouraged, he again began to spin around, hoping to see the rescuing shore. And he was surprised! The dark lines of the ground were directly before him, as far as the eye could see. But it still remained very far away. Still, it was the coast. The old man strained and swam with an obviously clear aim ...

It was absolutely bright, though the sun had not yet ascended, when he crawled out of the sea. Half a kilometer away, right on the sandy beach, stood several little tourist tents. The old man shouted, but only a hoarse sound came from his chest.

His legs buckled, and he fell with his face in the sand, unable to utter any more words. He did not remember how he was moved onto a sheet, how they rubbed his body with vodka, and gave him a drink from a flask. He drank, not waking up. Only in the evening he opened his eyes and began to regain consciousness. He was fed fish soup. Night fell again on the shore, and the kind "savages" (as the locals referred to the beach-dwelling tourists) carried him by car to the hotel where he had stopped the day before. His room had been cleaned. All his things lay how he left them. He opened the nightstand. There among the unnecessary papers was the passport in which he had enclosed a short note. "Please do not search for me. Do not waste your efforts in vain. I was born on the sea and decided to remain in it. Consider this as my will. I loved this world, but have not managed to integrate into it. Forgive me all, and farewell ..."

The old man lay down on a pillow and plunged into a deep sleep.

The next day, exactly on schedule, the airplane took off on the runway. Soon the sea appeared. The plane tipped down its wing and made a semicircle. Odessa quickly disappeared in the thickness of clouds ...

***

Part 3

Exodus

Serge lies half asleep. His eyes are closed. In the fireplace are nearly burned logs, and dim patches of light run across the walls and up to the ceiling. Sometimes he opens his eyes and takes a long look at the play of the yellow-orange tongues of flame. Then, he closes his eyes again, and he is instantly carried away there, to the Black Sea coast ...

The hot Odessa summer was replaced by the coolness of early autumn. The foliage on the trees was still green, but here and there, thin strokes highlight the yellowness of another time of year. A few more weeks will pass, and the crowns of maples and poplars will change their color to red-brown-yellow. Only the cypress trees shaped like candles will remain the same, proudly meeting winter's bad weather.

But now everything, except for puffs of colder wind, was still summer-like. The center of the city was overflowing with foreign tourists preferring the velvet of September to the stuffiness of August. They sat in small street cafes, slowly wandered around Deribasovskia Street, and were languidly interested in souvenir shops. It was the same as it was many years ago. Flocks of youth gathered, but only now their conversations were often interrupted by the various warbling of cell phones—nothing could be changed: on the Earth the 21st century was strongly affirmed.

Two days ago Serge and Janna arrived in the city of their youth. The circumstances of their meeting are not so surprising: in our century it is possible to fly from different parts of the world and arrive at one point. The surprise was something else—they met as if they had separated only yesterday ...

***

From the time of their last meeting in 1985, a whole eternity had passed. When in 1992, Serge learned that Janna, with her daughter and her mom, had moved to the USA, it became clear to him: in this life he would never see her again. He had already lived without her for about twenty years. The kids were growing up. Sometimes, it seemed to him that he was quite happy, but the number of nasty days was increasing. His business was falling apart. In his personal life his hopes for a solid foundation, between a man and a woman on which family relationships are based, never appeared. His wife, often without visible reason, created arguments with shouting and tears, and these do not promote a loving relationship. For weeks on end, Serge found it difficult to remove himself from a state of catalepsy and detachment. A feeling of loneliness engulfed him for a long time. Several times in the past years he opened the journal with his memories of 1973, and each time, tears welled up in his eyes.

He was continually putting away his journal, thinking that he would not open it any more. But then he was finding it again, and again was wiping away tears. That feeling for the woman which he experienced in 1973 never returned to him. For sure, he had affairs. But these affairs were fleeting and superficial. The birth of his children strengthened in him the thought that the past should remain in the past, where it belongs. He begged God to grant to him love for the woman, the mother of his children, and from time to time it seemed that God heeded his requests. But the Almighty handled it differently. He had not given happiness in home life to Serge, nor, as it became clear later, to Janna.

***

"Well, hi." Serge opened the door of the taxi and gallantly extended his hand to the lady. She fluttered out of the cab without effort as though her shoulders did not feel the load of the years lived.

"Hello," she pronounced with a smile and immediately fell silent, as if her lips were under the power of his. Then she smiled with the same wide smile, showing the whole expanse of her strong teeth, and a sparkle of mischief appeared in her eyes. Her black, big-bellied suitcase travelled into his car. At the beginning she was holding her purse on her lap, and then she populated the dash, just below the windshield, with her phone, cosmetic bag, wallet, and a bottle of water. The purse fell under her feet—she quickly arranged her spot, surrounding herself with things familiar to her. It seemed to Serge that she had been riding with him her whole life. The wall which had been built from a huge number of days apart collapsed: beside him sat that very same Janna, his Janka,[42] from the distant 1973 ...

Truthfully, to think and say *his* was presumptuous. But all the same he thought it, though he did not speak—he simply felt the warmth of a dear person. Ahead, the chain of cars facing the customs post appeared, and Serge tapped the car's brakes to take his place in line. He threw off his seat belt and drew Janna to himself. They kissed for a long time, as if they didn't finish kissing then, in 1973, and now it was necessary to make up for the lost time.

***

---

42 Janka—term of familiarity, like Mikey for Mike.

... Serge rises on his elbow, looks at the fireplace, and reluctantly gets up and throws on two logs. Then he takes the poker and moves the fire wood so that it doesn't burn too quickly, looking as if it were melting, although this may not be the right word.

He moves to an armchair and pours some cognac into the bottom of a glass. "My God!"—he thinks, "How fast these ten days flew by where we tried to replace our missed life together." And now again a separation—would it be another long time?

***

To find Janna in the presence of the World Wide Web was not so complicated. He had quickly found her on the Internet and sent an empty email, attaching only a poem he once wrote for her. That's all! He waited for a response. Then he stopped waiting—four or five months passed. Janna was silent. Probably, she had crossed him out of her life. So thought Serge. Maybe, she was right. Who was he for her now, 35 years later?

And suddenly in the list of received messages in his inbox—was her letter. Only one line: "My mom is dying."

Correspondence started, then communication by phone and Skype. Later, she told him that she would be travelling to Europe, to Romania to visit relatives, and this would happen soon. Serge suggested that they meet. Janna resisted for a long time, but eventually agreed to meet. Serge did not know whether there would be a continuation of this meeting. He simply wanted to see the woman who was so strongly burned into his memory. He also wanted to see for himself if the ending in 1974 was a fatal mistake or not. Maybe he was moved by simple curiosity. Maybe he was hoping for a continuation of the romance, so ingloriously and foolishly broken long ago. Some similar expectations gripped Janna as well, though she was afraid of this reunion. She was afraid to lose the bright memories of 1973. Without any ambiguity, she told him about it by phone. But both understood that most likely, there would never be another chance. And life rapidly counts years. They agreed to meet in Tiraspol,[43] in neutral territory, and then dash away to the Black Sea ...

***

"Why did you dump me, Seriozha?" She sat at the open door of a balcony and spoke as if to the street, where the yellow specks of autumn already filtered onto the dense greens of the trees. "Why did you dump me? What a blockhead! What have you done?!"

Serge lay on the bed and looked at the ceiling ... and what, really, could he answer? Yes, back then he was fainthearted, and he gave others the opportunity to convince him that he did not need this girl. It has already come to pass, it congealed with time—nothing can be changed. Why return, why look back? It is important to look forward, at what has not yet come to pass and at what may happen. He needed to think of the future, and whether they would have a joined future.

When she was tumbling down the rabbit hole, there in the past, it seemed to Serge that she would never return: neither in the present, nor in the future. He was afraid of this—he was extremely afraid. He felt like he was a billiard ball in a high-stakes game, and that now she would recoup her losses. She would take her ball and strongly

---

43 Tiraspol— is the second largest city in Moldova and is the capital and administrative centre of the de facto independent Pridnestrovian Moldavian Republic.

and precisely drive it into the pocket, so it could never roll anywhere again.

But she was coming back. Again she appeared in his embraces and spoke tenderly, with the low voice of a strong woman who wanted to be weak. She gently kissed his palm, and words of love flew from their lips that were pressed against each other ...

***

... A lone tear slides down Serge's cheek and falls into a glass of cognac.

"In 1974, whom did I make happy when I put the signature on this ill-fated paper stating that our married life has come to an end? Whom did I free? And from what was I freed? Myself? The anarchy of the following years testifies to it. Her? And how much happiness did she have for these past 35 years? As she said, very little." Both of them tried to find replacements for each other. Oh, what terrible nonsense, bosh, absurd! And though they agreed not to move back this marker on the scale of time, the idea was difficult to maintain—again and again it returns both him and her there, in this black 1974. But he doesn't want to think of it any more. He, despite his mature age, wants to look into the future, aspiring to grab what he lost earlier. Why? The answer is simple: because he, in spite of everything, kept his love for her.

"Yes, I love her very much!" whispers Serge, and tears drip from his cheeks. He picks up the glass, then looks at it and with one sip, drinks it down ...

***

"You left," she began. "Perished. Disappeared from my life. As though you never existed. But there is a memory, and from it I will never escape. I could not run. The first years after that foolish divorce I saw you everywhere: in the bus when I went about my affairs, in the street I found your image in passers-by. I looked in the faces of other people, but saw your face, or more truly, tried to see the features of your face in the faces of others. It was intolerable. You were next to me all the time. But the real you was not there. The most horrible thing began at night. I remained alone, alone with you, and still by myself ... I understood that it was possible to go mad. And it seemed to me that it had already begun. That reason had grown dull. And when there was a person who admitted that he fell in love with me, I surrendered. I wished to start living from a clean page. To leave you in the remote past. The new life has begun with the birth of my daughter—Allochka.

"But soon everything repeated. I could not embrace him, unless I imagined that I was embracing you. Somehow by itself, the formula of life worked out: let reality happen whatever, and in my soul I will live in 1973 to protect that, which we did not manage to save in reality ..." She sipped her already cooled down coffee. In the street were cheerful, chirping birdies. The easy sea wind swung the branches of the trees. In the end of September in Odessa, autumn was only beginning.

"Why did you dump me?" She did not cry any more, but she moaned. Then she became quiet for a long time.

Serge was silent as well. He lay on the bed and imagined that it would always be this way. Or at least, for a very long time. This return to the past, to 1973, would be here next to him, like a ghost. Wherever they would be, or wherever they would travel—it, 1973, materialized and took the shape of a phantasmagoric monster. But in fact, back then no monster existed. There was the love of two young beings. It was pure, without any platitudes or catches, just the attraction of two hearts. There was pleasure. There was happiness, at last. Why couldn't their long-standing relationship of 35 years be called happy? Then why recollect that period with such bitterness? No. Bitterness certainly, that all this did not continue. Everything was artificially interrupted, like an interrupted pregnancy. The embryo had not developed into a robust and strong love lasting the rest of life ...

Serge looked at his friend. In front of him was sitting an adult woman who lived somewhere and somehow without him all these long years. She was a stranger, but at the same time, absolutely close and dear—the same lips, nose, ability to laugh and cry almost simultaneously. He was looking at her. Her sight was aimed through the open door of the balcony somewhere afar. He brushed away furtive tears, but they again and again appeared in the corners of his eyes ...

"We can drive ourselves to the point of madness if we constantly torment ourselves with that divorce. I was just twenty-one. I was just a lad. How could I know that you can never be replaced? Yes, periodically it seemed to me that I was forgetting you. I was infatuated by others, like any normal man. But it quickly cooled down because, among other things, love requires being entwined. Not a unification of bodies, but of souls. My God, why do I spin this banality? ... Listen, you took a drink, and the coffee went down your gullet. And this movement is now congealed in the past. It never will return. You have another sip. But this one will be a different one. Not like the previous one. But the old one, you cannot repeat. It has petrified, like stone. You cannot do anything with it.

With our divorce, you cannot do anything, understand, my dear. Nothing can be done with the years lived. It is already history. While we live, it is necessary to look there, where we are capable to reach what we desire. Well, how will we benefit if we kill ourselves with our efforts and expire with tears for that, which you cannot return, and that, which you cannot change? ... Fie, with clever words I speak common truths, like an elementary school teacher. Forgive me."

"I want to eat. And, apparently, we can do something about it." She smiled, and cheerfully looked at Serge. She then set aside the cup and friskily moved next to him in bed ...

An hour and a half later they sat in deep leather armchairs at the restaurant, and assiduously studied the menu. Serge didn't feel like eating. He struggled all the time with feelings of stupidity that stuck to him from the irrevocably lived years outside of and apart from this woman. Though if he tried to undertake the slightest effort ... Oh! To hell with the elementary school teacher! To hell with all this mean theory. You simply tossed aside the whole thirty five years of pleasure to be near this matchless, unique, unpredictable in her actions and consequently an extremely attractive woman. Here she is smacking her lips and stops on a fish dish. Well certainly, Serge will eat fish too. To be at the seashore and not eat fish—what an absurdity.

"How did you manage to finish American graduate school in a couple of years?" he asked her. "You studied in a foreign language."

"Do you want to hear a joke?" Janna says. "Two Englishmen, two Italians and two Jews were stranded on an uninhabited island. After a while they were rescued. 'So, how did you live without women?' the rescuers asked the Englishmen.

'We are Puritans—we were never introduced,' was the answer.

'And you?' they asked the Italians. 'We established a schedule: one week I am the woman. The next week—he is.'

And then, there on the island they noticed two women with the Jews. 'My goodness! How did they get here?'

'It was difficult, but we managed to get them,' answered the Jews.

"Well isn't that funny? And I finished my degree the same way!" Janna burst out in laughter, and both she and Serge dipped their heads into 1973 ...

***

From the fireplace, orange light jumps out. Serge looks at a photo. It is dated 1982. A young woman ... An open face ... Her eyes are sad. As though they were inquiring: Am I alone? It's difficult for me. And where are you, man of mine, for whom I still continue to wait? Behind her on the wall—is a portrait of Hemingway. This is their favorite writer. He looks at the woman, as though he wishes to tell her what ordeals lie ahead of her. She does not know yet what she needs to overcome. There are still six more years before 1988, and the beginning of her difficult wanderings. In front of him is her photo with the sad beautiful eyes. This picture has been around for many years. The same amount of time will pass, perhaps, or less, and the one who now looks at her photo will no longer be here. And the photo remains as a frozen moment of life. Even though the photo paper already turned yellow, it is capable of telling much about the destiny of the person who is captured there. Paleontologists can use hardened bones to reconstruct the whole world from the depths of millions of years. But the photo of a person is only a representation of their appearance. Something else is still needed ...

***

"How did you end up abroad?"

"Um. It is a long story."

"So tell me. We are not rushing anywhere."

"Where do I begin? Probably, where my friend instilled in me the need to leave." She was deep in thought, frozen, staring at one point as though drilling through the layers of years that piled up since that time. Serge took a sip from a glass of fragrant wine and began to listen ...

***

We had a vacation in Koktebel, or Planerskoie as it was known at that time. The vacation was coming to the end. But we didn't want to leave. Alla and I are walking down by the seaside, and suddenly—Boris's lanky body comes into view. His face is covered with big dark glasses. Wow! I didn't know that he was coming here. And not by himself, but with his wife and children. Boris sits with me in a tent under the trees. They arrived at the sea unexpectedly. Here comes his wife Marina. She is kindness itself. My impression is that she loves all people in the world. We embrace. She brought two big buckets of almonds in green shells.

"What is this for?" I ask.

"For the winter," answers Boris.

We remove the green shells from the almonds and toss the nuts into our mouths. The almonds obviously will not survive until winter. We are going down to the sea together.

Dolphins swam along the coast. Very close. About a hundred-a hundred and fifty meters from the pebble beach. The vacationers' faces were turned towards the sea. Each time when the graceful animals jumped out in an arch and again entered the water, an approving rumble swept over the crowd on the beach. The dolphins, as if they knew, gave the people pleasure and carried out acrobatic jumps, like for an encore.

It was difficult to recognize how many of the creatures swam. Now they appeared, now they disappeared, but swam a straight course towards the cape of the Kara Dag Mountain, on the right side of the Koktebel bay. The dolphins brought that finishing touch, without which this picture of the surrounding nature would be incomplete. Little whitecaps covering the sea, the soaring seagulls, ducks diving, swimming, bobbing on the smooth waves; people, sprawled under the rays of the hot sun and splashing in the warm water, the hills surrounding the gulf—all this was united into an ecological system where only dolphins were absent. And here they appeared. Everything somehow became ordered, it became peaceful and cozy.

Alla and Elina, Boris's daughter, looked at the dolphins with open mouths. They squealed and jumped on the pebbles, echoing the jumps of the sea mammals. The adults smiled, looking at the children. For them, the grownups, this visit to Koktebel was a farewell. They knew it. But children did not guess anything. They only started to learn about this complex world, but did not suspect how complex it was. "And thank God!" thought the adults, looking at the loudly laughing girls.

"Mama, mama! Look, how nice they are, these little dolphins," Allochka cried out sonorously, clapping her palms together.

Boris placed his three-year old son on his shoulders so that the boy could see better. The child turned his head back and forth and did not understand what was happening. When he looked to the sea, the dolphins disappeared, when he turned to his father's face—they jumped out from the water.

"Whewe awe the fishes, the fishes, daddy?" The boy had trouble saying his 'r' and it sounded like something between an 'r' and a 'w'.

"Right there, look!" Boris pointed with his hand, but his little son, apparently, did not see anything. However, he also felt good, at least for an opportunity to sit on his daddy's shoulders.

The sea beauties swam away and did not come back. It seemed that they came to say goodbye to us.

Koktebel, during the Soviet time called Planerskoie, was a place for meetings and vacations of the representatives of the caste considering themselves the intelligentsia. Here, they got acquainted, went off in groups, then parted, and in a year or two gathered again. They brought along friends and girlfriends, and those in turn did the same. So the glory about the wonderful corner, created millions of years ago thanks to the eruption of the volcano Kara Dag and spiritually enhanced by the works and the philanthropy of Maximilian Voloshin[44], spread around. He has been captured by a naturally occurring bas-relief of rocks in the image of his profile on Kara Dag, and forever sleeps on the top of the mountain Kuchuk-Enishar.

Here at the beginning of the 20th century the artists

---

44 Maximilian Voloshin - was a Russian poet and famous Freemason. Voloshin's small village of Koktebel in Southern-Eastern Crimea, which inspired so much of his poetry, still retains the memory of its famous poet, who was buried there on a mountain now bearing his name.

and poets created their works. To make it easier for them to create their art masterpieces, the Soviet officials established "The House of Creative Activities for Writers," isolating it with a high fence.

In the silence of the shady avenues, placed into separation for better fertility, the members of the USSR Union of Writers bore their opuses. They, these members, drank vodka and young Crimean wine, played poker and chess, believing in their exclusiveness. In fact, their creative beginnings were guarded by a high fence that protected them from the rest of the world.

Diligent officials could organize any phenomenon, and to bury the spirituality of Koktebel—did not take much hard work. Why, in fact, preserve the history embedded in the name itself? To hell with Koktebel! Planerskoie[45]— here is the name of the resort! In fact, it was here on the mountain Uzun-Syrt that domestic gliding began. Yes, it is true. But why are technology and artistic creativity opposed to each other?

Representatives of the intelligentsia crawled through the fence to the House of Writers to peek at the writer's bodies and to "touch their artistic essence." Actually, it's curious: suddenly you catch a luminary whom you couldn't meet anywhere else. But the "luminaries" were hiding in small house-incubators and hatched best sellers. The intelligentsia neighed in satisfaction.

The days flew cheerfully in Koktebel. In the evenings we gathered at Anna and Vladimir's home, local residents who provided simple living for people on vacation. We

---

45 The original name Köktöbel in Crimean Tatar means "land of the blue hills." Its Soviet name of Planerskoie comes from the Russian planer, or glider: the hills above the shoreline were the site of many early experiments in manned heavier-than-air flight by Russian pioneer aviators. The local airfield is still known as Planerskoie.

sang songs with a guitar, told jokes, laughed a lot, drank plenty, and ate heartily.

"It is time to split." Boris said.

"You've only arrived! Why do you have to leave?" I asked.

"But not in this sense ..." Boris stretches his words in thoughtfulness. "There is no place to come back to, as a matter of fact. Before our departure from home, someone scratched a cross on the door of our house. Do you know what this means?"

"No," I answer.

"It means, that we are marked by these thugs— nationalists. Nobody stops them. Not law, not government, not militia. Tomorrow a battle cry will resound: Beat the Jews! And the Holocaust will begin with a new interpretation. And the most repugnant thing is that at work they hint to me about another nominee for my position. Fortunately, they let me go on vacation. They even paid me money. But I think it is just a tribute to good manners. When I return, they will show me to the door."

Boris broke off, filtering sand through the thin palm of his hand.

Boris is my close friend since childhood. He is handsome and very smart. Boris knows everything. Even when he has no answer, he all the same knows everything. I knew too, that in Moldavia anarchical forces were rising. They are gathering in parks and plazas, crying out chauvinistic slogans: "Moldova—for Moldavians!" All the others—Slavs, Jews and other ethnic minorities, should in their opinion, leave the country. But I did not give it much thought: they were just youth gatherings, I thought, nothing more ...

"Hitler's Germany began with street processions too. And then six million Jews went to the gallows and to the gas chambers. To leave, it is necessary—you understand, Jannoshka? Or are you immune? Maybe you have documents of a Turkish citizen?"

"Where to split to, Boris?" I whisper.

"Where? Probably, to Israel. Where else can you split?"

"And what will you do there?"

"I want freedom. I want to live easy!" Boris stands up and with long steps goes to the sea.

In fact everything is so good: the hot sun, the sea. What slaughter? What gallows? But, in fact, Boris said that. And he knows everything.

"Marin, what do you think on this occasion?"

"I think like Boris,"—was the short answer.

It was August, 1988.

In the sky there are no clouds.
The soft sea caresses the coast.
A dark profile hangs above the smooth surface of the sea.
It goes downwards from the rocks of Kara Dag.
Koktebel, my lovely, my dear, you are of Valoshin sunrises joy.

So the poet Yuri Yezersky wrote. I remembered it. So why don't people live in love?

***

At the end of the eighties, in the gatherings of the Moldavian nationalists in Kishinev and other cities of Moldova, appeals began to sound for the mass deportation of all "newcomers." Anti-Slavic and anti-Semitic moods amplified, and the Moldavian government at that time took the course of creating a mono-national state and seceding from the Union of Soviet Socialist Republics (USSR). People who lived in what eventually became the Prednister Republic were stirred to action against the militant national-fascism. Then the governmental circles of Moldova relied on using the rising contradictions among the population to keep control. Numerous attempts at a solution began in 1990 by using physical force on the Prednistrovian problem, and led to innocent victims among the peaceful population. The apogee of violence was the civil war unleashed by Moldova in 1992. More than 800 people ended up dead, and about three thousand were wounded.

It seems Boris really did know everything ...

***

September comes. And while the students are at the collective farms,[46] once every five years the college educators must take classes to improve their professional skills. *What else can they teach me? I got so many awards for being one of the best teachers in town,*—I think, but there is no way to get out of those classes. It would be better to stand at a chalkboard instead, but who will allow me?

The courses begin. I am at the last desk sharing the space with a twenty-four year old girl. My eyes are looking

---

46 Collective farms—every autumn the students had to go to the collective farms to help with the harvest.

forward. She is so bright! I am ecstatic about what she says! We think so alike!

The girl arrived from far away. I offer to let her stay at my house. Her name is Alla. Same as my daughter's. We become great friends.

I share a lot about myself with her. About my first love—that is, about you, Seriozha. She listens attentively, looking at my face. Everything interests her. And it is interesting to me to talk to such a listener. She understands everything. To me, it is pleasant, and I'm delighted that I am not keeping everything that has become painful inside.

"Alla, it is boring here for me," I told her one time. "It would be great to get away somewhere." She nods as a token of agreement.

I call a friend in the government entity on tourism. I ask her how to expedite a last minute travel package, and where I can get one—let me know, please.

"Good," says Nina. The conversation is over. Now I live with one thought: "When will this happen?" In the evening I get a call from Nina: "In two days there is a package to Yerevan. It's a great one. Do you want it?" My goodness! Yerevan! I had never been there.

A few days after my return, I leave the house and I see a sign on the door: a six-pointed star. I shudder. The fear, terrible animal fear, has gotten into me. A Jewish neighbor woman, who had lived in Kishinev since birth, tells me she has the same sign on her door.

Boris was right: it is time to split!

***

Urgently, I fly to Moscow. Lina, my girlfriend, hospitably receives me into her house. My purpose was almost unattainable: I needed to receive a visa to go to

Israel. But to leave Russia, you need to have an invitation from the other country. The invitation should come from close relatives. But I had no close relatives in Israel. I learned that the Israeli consulate does invitations, if your documents are in order. I approach the Dutch embassy where there is an Israeli consulate. The Soviet Union had no diplomatic relations with Israel, considering that this state was a stronghold of aggression of the Middle East. This is why the Israeli consulate was found in the building of the Dutch embassy. Behind these closed doors, I can obtain freedom. But so far, it is elusive.

There is a crowd of men. Only men. They look at me, look and probably think, "What is she doing here, where can she get through?" A fierce cold. Everyone stands. Everybody waits.

The crowd of men is my first obstacle. Who will let me pass? Everyone waits, like someone is going to bring them a bowl of hot soup. And who will get it?

I want to shrink and run away. But I do not do it. I cannot walk away from what I envisioned. In fact there was just one step, certainly a hard one: but if I get into this building—I have freedom. This thought simply eats up my brain. My body shivers a fine shiver. I have to get a hold of myself, because I need to think of something. But I cannot ...

At the embassy gate there were two guys in military uniform. They protect another's border, but maybe also their own. A young man approaches me from the crowd. "Do you have an exit visa?" he asks. "If you do, then they will let you in."

"What visa?" I answer. "I do not even have an invitation. I need an invitation. That is why I'm here. How can I see the consul?"

"This is impossible," the young man replies.

"It is impossible to get in there. I am in refusal,"[47] he says. "I have been here for two years and cannot get in. But there is one chance. The consul leaves for dinner exactly at one thirty. I know him, I see him every day. Everyone surrounds him at once: it is impossible to get close to him. You won't get through."

"But how can I receive an invitation?" I ask. "And what does 'chance' mean?"

"When he leaves, everyone stretches out their hands with notes containing their personal information. He takes them, and then you receive an invitation."

"Notes," I think. "And what if suddenly my note falls out of his pocket? Then what?"

"Well," I say, "we'll see. I need to see him."

It is three more hours before he comes out. The young man tells me during our conversation that the consul lives in the Ukraine Hotel, in room 245.

The young man is well-informed. It appears that he also lives in the same hotel.

"I think," the guy says, "the consul has lunch in the hotel restaurant. It is not far from here. Maybe 10-15 minutes by taxi."

In my head I carry out different scenarios of a meeting with the consul. It is not good to return home with nothing. Where would I go? Home, to Kishinev, to stay forever? But in fact, national disturbances and an orgy of violence had already begun there. What will meet me there? Horror, hopelessness, and no food in the stores. That means waiting would just be a struggle for survival, and I don't know who would win. And what if my mom dies? She is already many years old. She survived a war. She is a veteran of this war. She has awards and medals. And she could die from a stone

47 Refusal—when the Soviet Union did not allow people to leave the country. These people became dissidents.

thrown by any thug or punk. And my daughter! What can I give her, my Alla? She is already 11 years old. We live in a small house. How will we share one roof when she grows up?[48] Then suddenly a schoolmate will call her a kike again. And then again I'd have to catch this scoundrel and say, "If I hear this again, I will kill you. Convey this to your mother."

My Alla should be happy! I need to do everything so that she can always make her own choices. My words carried like an echo in my head. The shiver was gone. It was replaced by a mother's determination to struggle for her child. It was on an animal, genetic level.

My thought drifts to my mother. "Mom. My precious ... stay calm. It will be good for you there. Mom, the earth is very small and if we move a little bit farther away from here, I will prolong your life. Mom, trust me."

The crowd of men seemed to become insignificant and was no longer an obstacle. Now I know for sure, that a conversation with the consul will take place, in spite of everything!

"Permit me!" I say loudly. Heads turn towards me. A female voice!? I think it stopped the consul, who was just about to leave.

"Well then, please! Allow me to pass!" In this voice there is no request. There is confidence. I'm here. I will speak with *You*. Now! And *You* will not tell me *No*"! I kind of pumped myself up with confidence. I gave myself a pep talk: "it will be the way I want it to be!" I looked at him, not turning my head. Everyone who appeared in my way, I dismissed, overriding any objections with a soft, movement of my hand. Did I hypnotize him? Probably not. But in my approach there was no hint of entreaty,

48 During the Soviet period, several generations stayed in the same house waiting for 20+ years to receive permission to get separate housing.

no request to stop, to wait for me. He was bribed with my resoluteness—in it there was an intrigue that forced him to stand and wait for me.

"What is the matter?" asks the consul, measuring me with his eyes. Here I recalled that I was a young and attractive woman. Facing me is the consul. But he had a small fault—he was a man. I could see a man of average height, dark hair with neatly cut temples—the rest was covered by a hat—and dark-burning eyes. They looked out with surprise and curiosity. Certainly, he understood that here, people ask for only one thing. He understood that I approach him not as a man, but as a consul. But when I come closer, his eyes become soft, and in the depths of his pupils the expectation of flirtation begins to shine. Instinctively I guessed that this condition needs to be kept until I resolve my problem.

"I need to speak with you," I answer, trying not to lose his gaze.

"Speak," he pronounced, putting on himself the mask of the consul and looking back at those around him. A pause comes. Silence is around us. Only wisps of steam came from the hot breath of people. If I tell him about the visa I would then and there return to my place somewhere on the edge of the crowd, and God would feel sorry for his trouble of sculpting me as a woman.

I look the consul straight in the eyes, but I see in him a man. I speak firmly, interrupting the tightened pause:

"I cannot talk here. It's too cold."

"Well," almost with a whisper the consul answers, "I will return at half past two. Wait for me."

I search for the young man with whom I spoke earlier. I need to share with him. Let him be happy for me. I can help him too. "Actually," I think, "why do I bother with him? I still have not solved my problems. What a character

I am, to stretch out a helping hand to everyone. He may not even need it."

He is standing, talking with a fellow of twenty-five years. I introduce myself. I tell them what has happened. "I will take your information for the invitation with me, boys! Everything will be fine!" I think.

"Maybe we should go to the Ukraine Hotel and find him at lunch? We can sit down at the next table and maybe we can talk to him there?" offered the first young man. Superb! Certainly, we will go. We will take a taxi.

In the taxi the first guy says that he has run out of money. The money order from Kiev is just about to arrive, so he does not luxuriate at the moment.

"Do not worry; I will pick up the tab for the taxi and dinner." The second guy immediately suggests splitting the charges with me, and I agree.

Passing down the corridor to a room of the first guy, a woman on duty threateningly informs him that he must pay for a broken night lamp. The second guy and I split the cost. Our companion has enough troubles. We come into his room. I hang up my shearling coat on the radiator, to let it dry slightly. (While I was waiting for the consul, I opened the door of the building across from the embassy. The door had a small window, and I could look outside and watch. I leaned next to a radiator on the wall, trying to get some warmth. I did not expect that my movements would cause a pipe disconnection, and hot water would run down the side of my coat!)

We go into the restaurant. But the consul is not there. Then we go to the buffet on the second floor. We will eat quickly and then quickly return to embassy. Certainly, there is enough time before two thirty. It would be good to return, just in case, a little earlier.

We buy some food, we eat, then we go to the room and I put on my shearling. And suddenly, there is a knock at the door. The first guy is surprised. "Who's there?"

"Open!" There are three men in grey coats. "Come with us! Your passports?" Oh God! What time is it? Our passports are handed to those men in the civilian clothes. I start TO SHOUT! "How dare you? I'm going to miss my flight!" One of them approaches the phone and dials the number of Moldavian KGB, reads the information on my passport... and gives it back to me. "There is nothing to worry about," he says, "You are clean like glass. You can go." The boy who went with us got his passport back too. "And you," says the *civilian* to the tenant of the hotel, "We warned you. Stop speculating with Rolex. You remain."

The young man and I are taken down a corridor, tightly gripping our passports, afraid of some new unexpected stop. But everything is good. The main thing is to fly out of this building and catch a taxi. Goodness! If only we can be on time!

We made it back to the embassy... "Has he appeared?" I asked someone who was tramping around because of the extreme cold. The negative answer calmed me and gave me the opportunity to catch my breath. And here is the car. My consul!

Goodness! He silently approaches me, embraces my shoulders, and conducts me into the embassy. His assistant (or his bodyguard) follows us from the right side. Hooray!

Freedom is almost gained! My partner in the incident hands a note to me containing his information. "Don't doubt, my friend," I say. "Everything will be as it should! I will pass him your note."

"What is needed?" the consul asks, once we're inside the embassy. He removes my coat and offers me a chair across from his. He is already in his professional role, and he understands that I am not offering him a meeting in a cozy cafe.

"An invitation," I answer shortly and firmly.

"Give me your information."

"My papers? Here they are. Please!"

"OK! What else?" the consul says coldly, skillfully playing the role of an important official.

"Here is more," and I hand the information for my friend Boris, his wife, and their two children.

"OK! Give it here. In half a year there will be an invitation. What else?"

"Here's more," I hand him a page containing the information of a young man, my new acquaintance. The page travels into the consul's hands.

Outside, a KGB soldier protecting the embassy asked at the gate, "Your passport, young lady?"

"I'm married,"[49] I heard myself say before I had time to think of what to answer. The young, not so skilled brain of the soldier began to chew on my phrase, but time had been won, and I disappeared from his field of vision. Everyone outside asked, "So, how was it?"

"Hi! Now, you are talking with me, dear men!" I go to a restaurant to have supper with the one who was most interested in my experience. Why does he need to know this when he already has the permission to leave? Who knows? I just want to eat ...

At the restaurant I tell him the details about the event. He listens. He asks a question: "When will the invitation come?"

"In half a year," I respond.

---

49 I'm married — During this time Soviet passports were stamped if a person was married. Janna pretended this was an advance from the soldier to avoid surrendering her passport.

"Half a year? Are you kidding! That's too long! You do not know what can happen in this country during that time! With horror, I realize, "That's true, I do not know..." We go to a pay phone near the restaurant, and we dial the number of the Ukraine Hotel.

"Please, connect me to room 245." They connect me. The number is silent.

"Maybe I should call that guy who lives in the Ukraine?"

"Forget it. He is a provoker. Here everyone knows him."

"What does he provoke?"

"He brings people, as though accidentally, to special services (KGB), and then they can use their limitless powers to shake people down until they find something." I recalled the scene in the hotel: "But they did not really shake me down. They released me immediately. This means, once I was hooked, there was nothing to find. I guess I was lucky. Ooof!" I exhaled. In this country a dirty, sneaky trick can come from any direction ...

The next morning, I went down to a pay phone, wearing a nightgown, a coat, and boots with no socks. It wouldn't have been good to call from Lina's house—who knows who could be listening, and what kind of trouble it could get her into? Again, I dialed the consul's number. "You may not remember me. I was talking with you yesterday ..."

"Of course, I remember. You are the teacher from Kishinev. Is there something wrong?"

"I need to meet you urgently. I leave today."

"OK! I'm going to the embassy. Can you be there at ten?"

"I can't make it in time. I am in Izmailovo. It is a long way, and I am not ready yet."

"That's OK. Then will one o'clock do?"

"Yes, but they won't let me in. There are soldiers there ..."

"I will wait for you outside at one o'clock. Do not worry." I arrived seven minutes past one. He stands outside waiting. The shoulders of his jacket are covered by snowflakes. He is a man. He came for a date. The consul— is now his minor role. He will do everything that I ask of him. This thought became firm in my brain. I easily follow him inside. Like yesterday, he removes my coat. I sit down on the familiar chair which has been kindly moved up by the man-consul.

"What's the problem?" he asks.

"My mother is sick. Half a year is too long."

"OK!" replied the man. "Show me the information again." I hand him the page.

"You haven't forgotten? I have a friend. He has a wife and two kids. For them, half a year—is like half a life..." The Consul called the secretary.

"Send a fax, urgently!" and the consul immediately disappeared. In front of me sat the man with a pleasant exterior, similar to the prodigal son. Probably he'd reached his limit of official duties. He wished to go to his motherland. There, it is warm and cozy. But his motherland is far away. But near him, sits a woman who radiates warmth and internal security and calmness too.

"Maybe we will go to a restaurant in the evening?" the man said clumsily.

"I have a flight." I softly answer and smile with the edges of my lips.

"Yes, you told me, I forgot. Probably, I will find you in Israel."

"Certainly," I answer with relief. "The country is small, and it won't be hard." But to myself I think, "In Israel, my dear, you will search for me for the rest of your life. I will not be there."

I had convinced myself that I needed to make my way to America. But that was my secret. I returned home, to Lina.

"And where is the consul?" my inquisitive girlfriend asks.

"What consul," I ask. "I do not understand you."

"But I thought he would follow you. Everyone sticks to you eternally. Well, how did everything go?"

"I think it couldn't have gone better. Now only the waiting remains."

I fly home. On my door, the mail box is twisted into the shape of an eight. It's scary! In one and a half months the invitation should come. These days will seem very long! I go to the post office. My former schoolmate works there. "When the invitation comes," I ask him, "please give me a call. I want to take a vacation abroad, and will bring back a gift for you." The invitation came in exactly in one and a half months. I do not know which played the bigger role— the decency of the consul or the testosterone in his blood. My post office friend received a gift before my departure.

The time came to say goodbye to the city where I lived all my life. "The city," I thought, "where I married for the first time for love—perhaps for the first and the last time. Where are you, my fair-headed young man? Farewell! Now, you are only in my memory. Will I ever see you again? No, now is already never—all my resources are exhausted. Farewell, my magnificent, kind and sympathetic friends. No one will see me here again." But the hope that they would see me did not abate. It lived in me, having hammered itself into a distant corner of my soul: weak, but still alive ...

***

At last, all the documents are ready. Visa support from Israel is the only means to cross the border. Boris' idea to go to Israel did not sit right with me. It is a small country which is torn apart by religious contradictions, and an environment of terrible threats from the Arabic countries. What will I do there? It is unknown to me. You cannot live just anywhere. You can learn almost everything about Israel in just a few weeks. But I plainly do not know the language. Many Jews in the USSR speak exclusively in Russian and do not study their native language—why bother? No. America: this is my goal. I have to reach it, at any cost.

The packing begins. Some things should be taken with us, and some things—sent in the container. It is good that a relative of my friend in New York agreed to accept my cargo. The rest—I give away to friends. Finally, everything is done.

In the kitchen, on the radiator hangs Alla's claret sweater with white patterns across the front. One sleeve, slightly twisted up, hangs down like a piece of ship rope. Perhaps the sweater guesses that its mistress will not pull it over her little body anymore to keep warm. The keys are given to Boris. He will distribute to relatives, friends and acquaintances as he is told: furniture, rugs, utensils, the remaining clothes—everything on the list. The sweater will pass to the wardrobe of the neighbor girl.

The train from Kishinev leaves at three o'clock in the afternoon. A taxi is ordered for half past two. Everything is ready. But where is Mom? Doesn't she remember that we need to leave at three? The hands on the clock inevitably move forward. We leave from the Soviet Union ... forever. As long as nothing stops us.

But where is Mom? I cannot leave without her. She will die here by herself.

Here she comes at last, 25 minutes prior to the train's departure. She gets in our taxi. Neighbors are all around us and it is clear to everyone that we are leaving to go abroad. To hide it any longer is impossible, but the truth is no longer dangerous: nobody can stop us!

"I was at the October Palace at a big meeting," Mom explains the delay. "I sat in the presidium. I am so glad that I was there! You should have heard how they welcomed me ..."

She wanted to relish the pleasure of respect for her once again. Leaving for another's society, she understood, meant no one would know her there. Maybe she wanted to strengthen herself for the future. "Before this," she continued, "I went to the cemetery to your dad. In fact, I said goodbye forever."

At the station there are a lot of friends. They help to bring our suitcases and bags onto the train. They kiss Alla. They kiss me. Flowers. Smiles and tears. Someone speaks: "When you leave—you will grow foolish. There is no need to struggle for life where you go." Naive. Everywhere you are, it is always necessary to struggle for life. But in some places it is a struggle for survival. And in the others work, though often difficult, is for the best life, for well-being and the feeling of your own dignity. Boris jumped into the train car—he was going to ride with us up to the border.

Boris is tall. He stands near me at the end of the train car trying to wipe my tears. My eyes—are level with the woven deers on his sweater. Soon the deers become wet. Apparently, they cry too. The train carries us away from the city where I grew up, from the city which I will never see again. The only thing that I have done lately is to make a huge effort to leave it forever. But here in the depths of my soul, something stirred. It is a weak hope that has had an effect: and maybe, sometime I will visit the places precious to my heart? But that hope is empty. Soon you too, hope, will fall asleep forever ... Tears do not dry up: I know that a huge distance will separate me from my dear people. From youth, these people become you, and you become them. And no one can ever replace them ...

I start to think about what I desire most of all at this moment, where I am freeing myself from the country where I grew up, the country that is my motherland. Is or was? I heard somewhere: the motherland is the place where you feel good. And for me it can only be good where my dearest people are. But they, these people, are not going, not the least bit, to where I go. I—go to the West. They remain far away, in the East. It means, all the same, that I am losing my motherland.

Suddenly a dream is born, to calm me somehow. It is not natural for a person to grieve for a long time. It is natural for him to be happy. He does not come into this world for grief ...

In my imagination appears a big oval table. It will stand in my new kitchen, in my new house in the new country. All my friends will gather around it. They will come together at least one time. If only I could celebrate with them like I did in earlier times and tell them everything that happened to me that I can now only guess.

What is actually going to happen is full of uncertainty.

Only the hope for the best moves me. Only hope justifies my responsibility for my mom and daughter. Where am I taking them? Will it be good for them? Yes, it will! I have to believe in this! Though, really, there is nothing else left to be done ...

***

In my memory, shimmers my last evening of swimming laps in the open air pool. It is dark outside. Piles of snow are all over. My trainer, Nina, is shivering in her winter coat. She looks down at the swimmers. Suddenly, I feel like sharing with her my decision. "Nina, I am leaving tomorrow. Today is my last day."

"Where are you going? You like this swimming pool so much. You won't find a better one. This one is so close to your home."

"Nina, I am not changing pools. I am changing countries."

"What will you do there? Where will you go? You don't know anyone in the world."

"Nina, I will train and teach, same as I do here."

I knew I would not betray my hope!

***

But the damn tears are rolling again. "Boris, we will never meet again! We will be in different countries. On different continents! You have said it is necessary to leave. I am leaving, but you still remain."

"Jaaannnnna, do not roar," he always says my name long, stretching out the 'N.' "I told you: all of us should go to Israel. Together, it would be easier. But you chose your route. This is your decision. Don't cry, goodness! In five years we will meet. You will see. Well, stop, wipe your tears."

***

Here is the boundary city of Chop. To enter the city a special permit is needed. The Soviet country liked to create closed cities—reservations where only specially selected people could live and work. And it is possible to visit such cities only with sanctions from special entities.

Boris does not have a permit into this city. At this station, everyone on the train has to disembark and wait on the platform while the train cars are lifted and put on narrower pairs of European wheels. The whole procedure takes a couple of hours. Sometimes days—it depends on the railway workers. But not everything depends on pure mechanics.

According to the rules, all emigrants from the train cars must leave with their luggage and go to a building in the station to stand on the cold concrete floor, where customs officers check everyone who was on the train. They will wait for the next train, which will come in two days. This is most likely arranged to enable the customs officers to have plenty of entertainment. They take away from the people everything that was most dear and treasured for years, and passed from generation to generation.

With no declaration of export, it is not allowed to leave the country! Goodness knows what kind of reasons can be created when the power is on your side. Defenseless people potter about below. As for laws, there are few. The country is on the verge of disintegration. And here are traitors, fugitives who drag off with themselves "treasures of the country"...

To stay for two days on a cold concrete floor is a gloomy prospect. My mom falls ill. So far, she only has a cold, but she is 76 years. If I remove her from the train car, then pneumonia is inevitable. In my pocket is $126 that I was allowed to exchange. We have bags—too many to count full of canned food, blankets, and other things. I carry everything with myself that can compensate for money. Bags with canned food are very heavy. I have no citizenship. I had to pay the government 700 rubles to sell my citizenship back to them so that I would be allowed to leave the country.

Boris grabs the trunks and carries them to the door. I go to the conductors. "Guys! What can be done, not to make us leave? My mom is sick and I have a child."

"Nothing," the boys say. "We have been on this route for several years. Everybody leaves. The visas are already collected. We gave them to the customs officers."

"Boris," I shout. "Put the trunks back into the compartment!"

"You are out of your mind," Boris was taken aback. But he drags the bags back. Then he takes off from the train car and hides behind a night train, so as not to be caught by the frontier guards. A person without the special permit is, at the minimum, sent to a prison cell with a long time to *figure things out*. For us, especially for him, this is not needed.

Everyone leaves. I come back to the compartment. Mom's and Alla's eyes are wide open in astonishment. "Mom," I say, "Where is your jacket with the medals? Well, lie down. I shall cover you." The medals spread everywhere up to her shoulder. "Where is the Valerian?[50] Where is the Corvalol?[51] Now! Quickly! I need to sprinkle the

---

50 Valerian—a widely used herb in Europe as sedative, migraine treatment or pain reliever.
51 Corvalol— routinely prescribed in Russia as a sedative and/or vasodilator (blood vessel dilator). It is frequently prescribed for cardiac conditions as well.

medication around,"—it has a very distinctive smell. I have to show that my mom is not well. "The suitcases—let's put them on the top shelf."

"Let them stay there." What else? What else can I think of to obtain security that they will not send us to this parade-ground for offenses?

The conductors approached again, trying to convince me that we need to leave for the platform, and do the same as everyone else has done. Behind the window, it is already November 30th, 1989. Cold, fierce. Dirty snow.

Into the open door of the train car comes a huge customs officer, or a frontier guard. With him is some white-headed witch with dirty hair. They check to see if everyone has left.

"What are you doing here? Do you need a special invitation?"

"I have a sick mother, an invalid of the war. She cannot leave."

"Well then! ..." opens the mouth of the white-haired witch.

"If something happens to her, the *Pravda*[52] will learn of everything. Tomorrow, in fact, there will be an article in it. She is a war hero, and a famous person. If you do not know her—that is your problem ..."

I didn't actually have any friends at *Pravda,* and no article would have appeared. But the small wicked creature stopped.

"Open the suitcases," she shrieked.

"You open it. It is your job." I told her with easy confidence, although I understood that I was asking for trouble. In this, there was power.

---

52 Pravda—the leading Soviet newspaper at that time.

The "lady" stretched out her hand to the top shelf but ... decided not to get involved with the suitcases.

"Well then! Open your cosmetic bag."

"Please." I said as I opened the bag.

She grabbed some gold earrings from the bottom of the cosmetic bag which were not identified in the customs declaration. One of my friends put them in my cosmetic bag at the station. They probably thought I could save them for a rainy day.

"And what is this? Why is it not written down?" she says.

"Well," I'm thinking, "now she will send us back."

"Ohhh!" I say, "It is not in the declaration? OK!" A sharp movement of my hand—and the gold earrings fly out the train window, previously left open by Boris, who always knew everything in advance.

The male customs officer demands that I lift my hands and place them on the wall above my head. He impudently digs through the pockets of my pink Finnish jacket. Then both of them exchange glances and leave the train. After a while, I hear rustling under the open car of the compartment. But to me, it was already uninteresting ...

The compartment still keeps the smell of Valerian and Corvalol. Mom lies in the pose of a fatally wounded fighter. The medals, of a *Participant of the War* and the *Order of the Patriotic War First Class*, contemplated that they performed their service with honor. The conductors look at me, their faces stunned by such an unexpected turn. One of them approaches and says: "This is the first time I have ever seen this happen. We have a bottle of wine." The train was put on the European rails. The people who vegetated at the station for two days come through the doors. Hungry, tired, sick, dirty.

Then, years later, someone asked me: "What is emigration like?"

"Emigration," I said, having thought about it a little, "is like war without the bombing. People behave as if they ran away from the front line. Emigration is the same as evacuation. Not in the depths of the country, but from the country itself ..."

The train car is filling up with the voices of children. The old people are being helped to get up the abrupt steps. They are bringing their battered suitcases. The train takes off. "And the visas? Where are our visas?" I suddenly thought. They were still with the customs officers on the platform! They took them away when the previous passengers left from the platform. And my mom and I are without documents!

"Our visas are with the customs officers!" I scream to the conductors.

One of them sharply pulls the brake lever, and the train stops, not having had time to speed up. The conductors inform the engineer. The train car opens, and the white-haired woman appears with our visas. With shivering hands, I take them and check whether they are OK, re-reading them several times. Yes, everything is in order.

The train gets back under way. Mom tries to fall asleep. I hug my daughter. "My precious! Forgive me for all the difficulty which I put you through. Forgive me, my little girl! Later, everything will be good. Tolerate it, my little big friend. After all, you believe in me. This will all be over soon. I do not know precisely when, my daughter. This will end, and you and I will laugh again. We will again joke with everyone who comes across our path. I love you, you know ..."

Ahead, is the night. Soon, Czechoslovakia. We will

successfully cross the border where the soldiers will admire and welcome us, and where the gloomy faces of the Soviet frontier guards will never be seen again.

One of the conductors beckons with his hand. There is a bottle on the table. There are some more stewards from other train cars. They drink for me. The feeling of pride for myself helps me to survive and live ...

***

At last, the intense, nervous crossing over the Soviet border is behind us. The train cheerfully clicks its wheels. I look around. The people who just left the country where many of them already lived half of their life, rush somewhere into the future. What it holds is not known to anyone—or to me either. I could only trust that it will be better than the past, and furthermore the present. Otherwise, there is no sense in it. The majority of my fellow passengers are married, middle-aged people. Everything about them is obvious: the husbands work all the time and the wives just sit on their butts. Spoiled, doing nothing, they continually demand their husband's attention for any trifles. "Get that small suitcase. I want to get a jacket, it is cool." And the man climbs to the last shelf, and from lots of things, fishes for the necessary small suitcase. 'Wifies'—for certain are specialists with diplomas ranking themselves as the intelligentsia. But whether they actually worked on their specialty or not—is an open question. Do they know anything at all besides spoiling their little doggies, which they hold in their arms and to whom they give more preference than to their kids and grandmothers whom they drag somewhere into uncertainty?

Next to me, sits a lady (she can only be called a lady because of her impressive weight). I get acquainted with her and her seventeen-year-old son. The lady continually teaches the child what is good and what is bad. The boy looks unusually kind and trustful: his big light eyes do not express anything except tiredness. His lips are chubby, like his mother's lips, and his light curly hair is like hers too. They are not so interesting to me, but there are no other fellow travelers nearby.

In Czechoslovakia there is another stop. We change trains. Everyone needs to leave. Boris remained in the Soviet past. He will not reappear now to easily pick up the suitcases and bags to rearrange them on the other train. We need to search for other assistants. Luckily, the seventeen year old boy jumps off the train and helps place our luggage on the new train.

Mom, Alla and I are standing on the platform. "Why does Alla's face look like an old woman's?" I wonder. She has somehow grown thin and matured during these days. "Goodness, what I have done!" I look at my mom and think how this lady, who was honored to dance with Boris Yeltsin, now, goes through such suffering.

At last we are in the train car. The train gets under way. Ahead is Austria. We still stand in the corridor. The mother of the boy moves ahead of me and sticks her index finger (covered by dry, badly-groomed skin) right into my face. Loudly and purposely she speaks directly to me: "And you do not forget what we have done for you!" What is this? What did she want to say? But her purpose is achieved: she insults me to tears. The boy tries to apologize to me, but it is already too late. His mother did her deed.

I went to the end of the train car. There I meet the other man who helped transfer our suitcases. He smiles—the mouth is full of gold teeth. He starts speaking, obviously trying to interest me: "Don't pay attention to the fact that I am short. I am so clever, that if you take some away, I'll still be clever. Here are some things that I have bought. Nested dolls, souvenir spoons, and several picture cameras. I made it possible to outwit customs."

He wheezed heavily. He turned away, seeing my full indifference to his bragging. Then he gained strength and continued: "In Austria, I will get rid of all this. I will get a pile of money. You know, there is a woman waiting for me in Kharkov. And in Italy too, there is an acquaintance ... She loves me, this is how!" He again breaks off and pulls out a cigarette from his pack. He takes a few puffs and suddenly jumps up to me and spits out a line, his mouth looking like a case filled with gold: "You know what? Just marry me! I see you are a lonely woman, overloaded—you have your mother, the child, suitcases ... But I will help you. You can rely on me. I am only here to get money in Austria, and we will start a good life ..."

I shudder and open the door of the train car. "You see, suitcases are temporary. At this time, I don't need a temporary husband. I'm sorry." His love for me somehow quickly dried up. He did not approach me anymore. In Austria, I remember, he displayed the knickknacks, and traded. Then he disappeared. I did not see him anymore.

In the evening, about ten o'clock, bodies in winter clothes unload at the Viennese railway station. Everyone goes up to the second floor. It is Friday evening. December 1st, 1989. It seems like an eternity has passed since we left Kishinev.

According to the chatter, we are supposed to be picked up. I heard it spoken about earlier, but not in details. In short, for some reason we begin to wait for buses. But nobody comes. About an hour passes, and suddenly through the loudspeaker comes the announcement: "Everyone must leave the station premises by 12 midnight. The building is closing."

"The doors will open again at six in the morning. Suitcases and hand luggage should be taken with you." Outside is frost, snow. There are more than four hundred of us. Everyone leaves. Suitcases, bags, my mom, my courageous girl—everyone is tossed out into the snow. The crowd buzzes and at the same time keeps calm in cold horror. Everyone obediently gets out. The snow falls. The crowd at the Israeli consulate pops up in my memory. It is strange: it appears that it is easier to control a crowd, than to control one person. The crowd has three states: it is obedient, or exults, or is enraged. But this crowd has arrived from the Soviet Union—it has gotten used to obedience. The organization which should have delivered the buses had simply forgotten about the arrival of the emigrants. The people helping the emigrants appeared to be Jews. And Friday is their sacred day. A holiday. Beginning of the Sabbath. Here they also enjoy their warm houses. This enjoyment will proceed until Monday. For everyone who arrived, this means that they must spend the whole night with their old men and women, children, and suitcases in the frost, until six o'clock in the morning when they will be allowed to move into the station building and enjoy the warmth until midnight.

I sit Mom on a suitcase. The sadness does not leave her face because she does not have the strength to stand up for her child. Alla looks as if she is bewitched; she does not take her eyes off me and tries to guess my actions.

"Daughter, guard everything here, and I shall run upstairs to talk to someone." The station is not closed yet, but I am the only one on the second floor. Where have all the strong men gone? Oh! All of them guard the families outside. Nobody even tries to understand, or to change the situation. If the order is to lie in the snow—OK! Crawl!

OK! Even when sent to the barracks, they also will go and not say a word.

I go upstairs. I search for the manager, the chief, director—anybody who can help. I did not sleep for two days. I cannot sleep on the road, especially in such turmoil. There is the managing director. I tell him about the situation that has developed.

He measures me with his eyes and negatively shakes his head. "No," I say, "you find me the phone number of these people. Now." In the railway station air, hang the words which are flying off my lips: emigration, Perestroika, peace to the world, freedom. He stops me and leaves, calls somewhere, and comes back. I'm so tired. I want to sleep. Things move so slowly ...

In half an hour there appears one of the bosses of the organization sponsoring the resettlement of the emigrants. He is tall and good-looking, wearing a chocolate colored leather coat, with a fur shawl-like collar that comes to an end near his waist. He is freshly shaved and wears expensive cologne. As I look at him, before my eyes arises a vision of a huge hall, women wearing fancy dresses with open shoulders, light from chandeliers, music, champagne, and chocolate ...

This one also measures me with his eyes after the station manager introduces us. It seems to me that he looks at me with irritation, and maybe squeamishness. Yes, I look like a vagabond. No, I did not take a shower for several days, did not wash my hair, and did not have a manicure. Yes, I am from that country which you do not love, and maybe hate. You think, why am I going to this well-groomed, refined society? You think, what am I here for? But you in fact know. Hell, you are helping us to move, which means that you are sure that we shall get accustomed, and we shall find human dignity. I am of the same opinion. If I could only take a bath ...

From a short conversation it is revealed that our friends supporting the emigrants in Vienna have simply forgotten that people would arrive on Friday. A cold apology—but in half an hour five Icarus buses pull into the railway station. Only women and children with their luggage are allowed to enter the buses: there are not enough seats.

The buses are gradually filled. The men remain on the platform. They will wait under the open sky 'til the morning when the other buses will arrive for them. Half of the family luggage remains with them. I enter the last bus. People settle freely, with comfort like they are going to a resort. "Well, scoot over: without me you would wander the railway plaza like cows all night long!" People are silently moving closer together. To accommodate Mom, Alla, and me they release some space on the long back seat at the end of the bus.

"Wait!" I shout to the bus driver. "I need another ten minutes."

I approach him and explain that all the men remain outside until the morning, like cattle in a corral. I will try to do something for them. The driver agrees to wait.

"Go ahead, just be quick about it," he replies in Romanian. Everyone who heard my conversation thought that I spoke in Italian. Actually, I spoke in Romanian. Nobody asked questions.

As fast as my legs would carry me, I run to the station and fly by the men who obediently accepted their lot to wait for morning. I fly through the still open doors of the station. On the second floor, again I search for the manager. I explain to him that for the first time, we have arrived in a civilized country, and are compelled to freeze in the cold, here, in the center of Europe. "This," I told him, "is a reproach to you and your hospitality." He listens attentively, maybe from politeness. But his face is like stone, and it is impossible to understand what is happening in the brain of this human. I feel like I am winding myself up, and I even choke with anger.

"There are sick people out there, and some with heart problems. By the morning you will have dead men on your plaza. Then you will have to talk, but not with me ..."

I glare at him, and saw that it worked: he picks up the phone receiver. It appears unsolvable problems do not exist: all the men with their suitcases can be moved to an electric train, which will stand at the platform until the morning. In it, they will be warm. Nobody will freeze, they won't get sick. I am full of impudence and I stretch my hand to the manager, but so that it is difficult for him to understand: for a handshake or for a kiss? The man hesitates, then takes my small hand into his big warm palm and gently shakes it. Then he does not withhold, and brings it to his lips. "You are a charming, courageous and persevering woman. Successes to you. Welcome to Austria."

I go, but I fly downstairs, light, like a helium balloon. In effect, men, totally unknown to me—will live through the night in warmth. I again run up to the bus, persuade the driver to give me a little more time, and come back to the station. In fact, nobody there speaks English. The crowd follows me with gladness. Everyone goes aboard the electric train. Everyone! Nobody remains on the plaza. "Hey! You at the station! Now you can close the doors!"

Again I am shifting everyone in the back seat of the bus. Next to me, a woman sits with her daughter and mom. In her hands is a little dog. The dog has a dry nose. Its mistress has decided not to spend money to buy her dog some water. "Alla, where is our bottle of water? Look, what a dry nose the dog has ..."

All the buses depart for different hotels. We are carried to northern Italy. At daybreak, at six o'clock, we approach the hotel located in the mountains. We are still in Austria, but extremely close to the border. The owner waits for us, and has prepared warm rolls for his visitors.

He is going to set the table, and serve tea. But on the sly, the crowd steals up to the trays with rolls. Some start to stretch their hand to the food. "Let go!" I order. "It is enough to embarrass me!" Hands disappear. Alla, Mom, and I receive a room, a big light room in a picturesque mountain hotel. At that time, we did not know that we would be fed two times a day, that everything was paid for, and that we would stay in this room for two whole months while waiting for authorization to leave Italy.

We take a shower and we lay down on the beds. A couple of hours later there came a knock at the door. I open it. "Tell me, and where is my husband?" The question repeats again and again with each new knock. I get up and hang a note on the door: "Your husband is not here. Pass by." All husbands are sitting in an electric train. Oh, to hell with them ... I put my head on the pillow—and immediately I plunge into the deep dream which carries me away from the reality of life into some fairy tale.

***

"Italy ... Oh, Italy! Though time runs rapidly, Italy will never grow old. The antiquity of this country only transfers the unique aroma of its youth. The charm of eternal youth is created by nature, the sea, and cheerful people ... But the everyday modern reality overlaps the breadth of History. The present, Antiquity, Revival, and the Renaissance have fancifully intertwined into the image of Italy, having made its Olympus of poets, artists, sculptors of all time: their Muse, their inspiration."

No one remains indifferent to the country! Millions of tourists stream to Italy like pilgrims, but for their short vacation they see less than a hundredth part of its sights. A whole life will not suffice to glance into all the corners of Apennines Mountains, where each stone can tell about the events that occurred during the long centuries.

Rome. The skeleton of the Coliseum. The all powerful Vatican—the center of the Catholic world. It is a small country squeezed into the Cathedral of St. Peter and the Papal Palace. The Vatican is the keeper of the Sistine Chapel—an outstanding monument to the Renaissance. Its walls and arches were painted by Sandro Botticelli, Pinturikkio, and Michaelangelo, which made the Chapel a masterpiece of mural painting.

At the gate of the sanctuary stand robust Pontifical Swiss Guards in their exotic uniforms. And crowds of inquisitive tourists wait for the truly theatrical changing of the guard.

The motley public mills about in the streets. Rushing cars and brisk motorcyclists dodge between them. Youth sit on numerous steps. Children are near the fountains. Actors entertain the idlers. The cafes, which have crept out onto the sidewalks, have begun radiating the delightful smells of espresso with air foam and cinnamon.

The Milan cathedral spins your head and takes your breath away. Time connected on a small plot of land the masterpieces of the gothic style, the Renaissance, a baroque of classicism, and modernism. Moreover, many architectural styles have arisen in Italy. Saturated by antiquity, they create the color inherent only in this country. A person wanders in the centuries, and in a second, penetrates the millennia.

The Leaning Tower of Pisa managed to bend in 1173 during its construction, and became frozen in time, for centuries. Galileo threw stones of different weights from its top, but did not explain why the force of terrestrial gravity had not laid the tower flat.

Verona, brought to light by the grace of Shakespeare, and the love of Romeo and Juliet …

Venice, rolling in water; magnificent buildings and palaces stand on 118 islands, supported by pillars made from the Siberian larch. Four hundred viaducts and bridges connect among themselves these small land patches.

Gondoliers cheerfully dash about on sea streets, exchanging words amongst themselves, like female traders in the Odessa flea market. They tell jokes and address the gaping mouths of passengers. "This is the house of Casanova. But to come nearer is not recommended for innocent girls."

There is always a congestion of people and pigeons in the plaza of St. Mark's. And everywhere cafes and restaurants sate the lovers of ancient exotics by the aroma of fragrant Italian dishes—the appetizers alone can come in ten variations of mussels and different culinary styles. All this creates the impression that the area is an eternal festival. The Rimini Resort has the widest beaches, on which ladies easily stroll in the evenings in light fur coats. And half-naked prostitutes walk the curb of the main highway wagging along the coast of the Adriatic Sea.

San Marino—a small country which has gone into the mountain, towers alone above the plain. There, you are treated with wine and fried meat. There, they sing ancient songs. In fact, songs are sung everywhere in Italy, and not only ancient.

Florence is the wellspring of painting. Here in a small space so many unique works of art are located, like nowhere else in the world. The historical center of Florence is easy to classify as a gigantic museum arranged directly under the open sky.

The motherland of the Italian pizza—Naples. The word 'pizza' comes from Latin 'pita'—a flat cake. Neapolitans themselves claim that the first 'present day pizza' was prepared in their city. Annually in Naples, the 'Pizza Fest' holiday is held. The best cooks fight for first place in preparation of this simple, but very tasty flat cake. The well-known 'Margarita' pizza was specially prepared in 1889 for the first queen of Italy, Margherita of Savoy.

It is difficult to believe that from the moment of the formation of the Roman Empire, two and a half thousand years ago, this nowadays cheerful country conducted terrible bloody wars, and with a handful of friends, Spartacus went into his last battle.

It is not clear why, in such a beautiful country, this was the last staging post for emigrants from the Soviet Union.

***

We—are not tourists. On us is the brand of refugee. Yet we are being helped. For this, many thanks are due to the Jewish communities scattered worldwide. They are united. And through them, the Jews living on the planet are all united. Altogether, there are fifteen million. Forty percent live in Israel. Thirty-five percent—in North America. The rest are in other countries, wherever they were thrown by destiny. And the destiny of Jewish people does not look like any other. It is a constant struggle for survival, continuing through the millennia. External aggression (it is enough to remember the Holocaust), oppression in the Soviet Union, and the permanent struggle against Islamic factions—all this promoted the rallying of Jews. Now, this unity is at a genetic level. Here is an example of the base laws of development of nature and society: action prompts counteraction.

The American Jewish community is powerful. The Presidential Conference unites the majority of the Jewish organizations in the country. After my arrival in America I talked to Joe Bettman—the ranking officer of HIAS, the organization which was engaged in our relocation and was responsible for all current expenses. "Why do you help Jews?" I asked. Wide-eyed, he replied immediately, "Jews should help Jews!" It sounded like an axiom, or a mantra like the Lord's Prayer. I even felt the foolishness of my question. Upon our arrival we received brightly lit apartment and warmth from the people who met us. They looked after us, as if watching over patients. But on the way to the U.S., my nerves had been stretched to the limit.

***

January 9, 1990. We are herded like animals, for the next stage, to the town of Ostia. It is not far from Rome, and is directly on the coast of the Mediterranean Sea. The rooms in comfortable hotels are not expecting us, the camp for re-settlers waits for us in the wet forest.

It's winter, but there is no snow. The air is saturated with moisture. Feet slide on the earthen trodden paths. The dirt is mixed with fallen down foliage, pine needles and wet snow. You try not to fall flat there. My mom—is a hero, not only of World War II, but of the emigration of the nineties. Only they don't give medals for emigration. She walks beside me, silently. It is her 78th year. She is strong. My daughter is younger than her, by more than sixty years. As a teenager, it is permissible for her to whine. But she, too, silently moves her legs and drags the luggage.

Here is the small house which is allocated to us. It is possible to have a rest, to sleep. How much I longed to sleep! What a miracle—to be stretched out on a cot and to plunge into a dream. Soon, soon it will happen ... We only have to wait for the guy who has taken our carts to transport our suitcases. He said that first he will transport his suitcases, then ours. The bus which delivered us did not go into the woods—it would simply get stuck—so we go on foot from the road. Mom has gotten acquainted on the train with the parents of this young man. She defines them as a decent family.

And here he is, our guy. Now we shall quickly reach the small house. But where are the carts on wheels? We bought them in the Soviet Union. You put on a suitcase, you pull the handle forward, and you drag your luggage. Well, anyway, a monument should be made to the inventor.

"I'm very sorry," the guy says, "but your carts are broken. Made in the USSR." He spreads out his hands with his palms up, as a 'what can you do when nothing can be done' gesture.

"Why the hell do I first help others," I mutter, "then suffer? It would be OK, if it was just me. In fact with me are my two most precious women. Why should they suffer because of me? I will give nothing to anyone, anymore. If you didn't buy it, then you don't have it—untangle your problem yourself ..."

To repair the carts is impossible. The wheels have flown off the axle. The guy left. Well, at least he is from a decent family! We transfer, no, we haul the suitcases by ourselves. They are dragged on the ground and turn into something unimaginable. You would need to use a spoon to take the dirt off. It is a joke from my youth. But now it is not funny ...

At last, we get into a small cardboard house. Well, it isn't actually cardboard—it just looks like it. It is made of wooden boards. It looks like a strong one, like it will not fall apart. However, there is no electricity. On one hand, there are shabby bunk beds and the walls are damp. On the other hand, there is a roof. And here is a small closet. There are probably blankets and pillows. Yes, dream about it—it's empty. We get our thin blankets that were packed just in case. Here, the 'case' became the reality! We try to fall asleep with Alla on one plank bed. But there is not enough room. Alla moves to one of the empty plank beds.

Mom is making herself comfortable on the bottom bunk, covering herself with a blanket and a coat. "Oh, Mom," I thought, "Just don't get sick. I need to deliver you to a new life, no matter what! Bear it a little bit longer, just a little more. We are together; we will not let you go."

Despite the cold, weariness prevails, and we fall asleep.

Morning. I open the doors and my eyes squint from the bright light. I need to procure some warm water. A young man passes by. The day before, I gave him my carton of cigarettes, having decided to quit smoking. But now, I want to smoke so badly—I can't stand it. The young man is puffing the cigarette with pleasure. Probably, my cigarette!

"Listen," I address him, "to immediately quit smoking, it appears, is not easy. Can I ask you for a cigarette, please?"

"A cigarette? Sorry, this is my last one." At the top of his breast pocket, a pack of *Stolichnie* cigarettes is sticking out, looking the same as when I gave it to him the day before. He was also going to America—a "pleasant" fellow traveler. Once again, I order myself: don't give anything to anybody! Let well enough alone. Have you forgotten that common truth? Now, go find a bamboo to smoke ...

Later, I meet a woman who rode with me by bus to the camp, the day before.

"Do you want to tag along with me to Torvaianica, and look for an apartment?" she asks. Certainly, I want to. Torvaianica—is a distant suburb of Rome. It would not be bad to rent an apartment there. And it would be easier to share it. We should leave the small houses after a week, tops, and move to rented habitations. These are the conditions. Probably, we are followed by the next party of emigrants.

We sit down on the bus and we go. Mom and Alla remain in the small house in the woods. If only they do not catch a cold, or fall ill—I pray.

We drive into a small, cozy town. All the houses are occupied. It seems the whole of Italy is flooded by emigrants. There are no vacant spaces. At last, maybe by chance, we find an apartment which we will share with the family of this woman. We will move there in two days. That is so great! We will have a shower! With this joyful news I hasten back to Mom and Alla. It is getting late. We searched for living quarters all day long. Unexpectedly, my fellow traveler and my future neighbor meets friends from Kiev and remains with them. But I cannot wait. I hitch a ride with a car. Someone brakes. I sit down. At the wheel is a young man. There is nobody else in the car. He doesn't speak English. And with Italian I have big difficulties. Using gestures I explain where I need to go. It seems he understands. Well certainly, this camp for refugees is probably known to the whole local population. The car is clean, and well-groomed. The guy is handsome, clean-shaven, and peaceful. I also become at ease and cozy in this car. I relax, and my eyelids close by themselves.

Suddenly, it becomes dark. We left the city boundaries, and the street lanterns remained behind. Relaxation was replaced by stress. We drive down a road framed by a dense wood. It becomes frightening to me. I ask the guy to turn around and take me back to the city. He does not understand, or does not want to understand. I begin to shout. But the sense of shouting is not clear in his language—he only shrugs his shoulders. Unexpectedly, he tears his right hand off of the wheel and reaches in the back seat. What does he have there? A Knife? A pistol? Animal fear takes over me. The car is borne forward, and the road lit by headlights, dives under the wheels. I have not noticed, and now begin to speak in Russian: "Please, stop, let's return ..."

He gets a cigarette from the pocket of his jacket on the back seat and hands it to me. "It is a maneuver," I think. "Now I will light it, get distracted, and he will knock me on my temple."

"Prego?" he says, "Emigranto Russo?"

"Dah, yes, yes, sí, perso-lost!" I confirm in all languages which come back to my memory. "The camp is in the forest."

The car sharply turns into the woods. Ahead, is a barely recognizable train crossing barrier. Around—infernal darkness. He indicates with a gesture that we have arrived. What if I get out, I worried, and he leaves, and I remain alone in the woods at night, in an alien country! But then, I saw a strip of electric light that made its way through the trees. I reach for the ignition keys and I ask him to escort me. "No, no," he almost screams. "I have a bambina, she waits for me, my bride." Here my fear sharply passes into impetuous, nervous laughter. I am simply doubled over in mirth. "My God, he thought that I was dragging him into bed to thank him for delivering me! He also laughs, though it isn't clear to me why. In any case, Soviet-Italian relationships have sharply improved ...

In two days, after we already began to prepare for leaving, the woman with whom we have rented the apartment enters our small house and declares that she has invited her friends from Kiev to live there instead. "And you, beg your pardon, should look for another place."

"But I actually found the apartment!" I shout in her face. "A guy approached me and guided us to the address of the rental."

"So what?" she answers. "You should not have left that evening. That night, my friends and I agreed and gave them the money."

"So why in the hell are you just now informing me about it?" I became enraged. My mom steps in, though: "Why worry? God spared us from living with such a neighbor." She looks at the woman and says, "Go, dear, we do not want to detain you anymore!"

After a while I manage to rent a room in the resort city of Nettuno. It is a lovely small town with numerous hotels. The sea is close—in a word, not the worst place to wait for the visa to America. In one of the plazas of the city, emigrants gather and discuss various problems. Somehow by itself, the information filters down from different sources. Who leaves for America and releases a room; or who on the contrary, is looking for it. In short, it isn't exactly a town hall meeting, but it is an emigrant meeting. I come every day ...

The room where we moved to is empty. There is only one folding cot. We place our suitcases around this cot—and turn it into a bed.

The walls are covered in mold, and the door of the balcony is always ajar. It is January. When we moved in, a kind gentleman, who was about to leave for America, helps us move our things to this room. He offers to deliver the rental fee to the landlord who lived across town. I am so thankful that someone is taking care of us. A few days later, he and his family left. That very day, the landlord says "Basta, immigrazione russa è finite!"[53] and throws us out in the street for non-payment of the rent. Same cold. Same January. Same suitcases to drag in the streets. How I found another apartment, I don't remember ...

***

Certainly, it would be silly to spend four months in Italy and not see some of the sights. Alla decides to show her dearest mom Florence and Venice. It was a three-day round trip tour, by bus. But it costs money. Where to get it? Definitely not from the organization which sponsors us, and which pays for the rental apartments.

Immigrants in Italy did not have permission to work. However, Alla learns that teenagers could earn additional money by washing the windows of cars at intersections. This "business" (to use the term loosely) began booming in the Soviet Union. Boys bought the workplaces, and

---

53 Basta, immigrazione russa è finite!—Enough! Russian immigration is done!

each "spot" was protected by a young fledgling gangster. Racketeering already squeezed into all cracks of Soviet society.

The same scheme was transferred onto the Italian ground. Alla buys a sponge, a brush on a stick, and goes to the intersection. But it is only possible to take a spot which is released, and that only happens if someone left for America. Such a spot is not available. I go with my daughter, I worry. On the other side of the street there is a man who acts as though he protects the group of teenagers. Alla stands up at her 'spot' and starts to wash the windshields of passing cars.

"Hey," the man approaches, "This spot should be purchased! And only then, when it's available. Is that clear?" Here, I interfere.

"It is quite clear, that you give direct gangster orders. This girl will work here! Now, is that clear to you? And if you try to interfere, the police will be informed as to how you are occupying yourself, here in Italy. Do you understand, unfortunate racketeer? You do not know who you're talking to ..."

The man was taken aback and left, as though considering a method of struggle against me. But he did not struggle. Probably, being fairly clever, he guessed that he did not desire a conversation in a police station: in fact, he too was waiting for a visa to the USA. From that day forward, Alla went to her "spot", as if going to work.

Using the money she earned, we really went to Florence and Venice. I will never forget this gift from my daughter, then a twelve-year old girl. She showed character and bravery, which she would use even more in her future life ...

A month later, we were flying over the Atlantic ...

Part 4

Return to the Future

The sleepless night spent at the restaurant tired both Serge and Janna. They only felt the weariness after the end of Janna's story. She was overwhelmed. It seemed for her that the present became the future, and the past became the present. She dove deep into her memories, and they swallowed her. She did not see Serge, and only sometimes turned to him and asked: "Do you understand?" But more likely, it was a certain attribute of the story, rather than the desire to find out if he understood something or not. Serge only was ordering: wine, water, or ice cream. However, the last was only for him. Janna did not eat ice cream. Serge had many questions, but he did not break her monologue. What for? Somehow later he figured he would get the details. He knew that he would not hear a smoother and more consecutive version of the events of her story. And details can somehow be clarified, without being imposing.

Janna broke off. She sat for a long time, almost not moving, still somewhere far away. "That's it, Serge, my head hurts. Let's go."

It was almost five o'clock in the morning. There were almost no visitors. Night had ended, and the restaurant was closing. They paid up and went across the street—to the hotel room. The coolness of the morning refreshed them. They were standing at the entrance, enjoying the crystal air. Then they went up to their floor. Janna quickly took a shower and climbed under the blanket. She nestled next to Serge and closed her eyes. After a while, her easy breathing announced that she was already in the land of Morpheus. They slept long. Almost until noon. Just like a long time ago in Kishinev. Their stay in the hotel, they decided, should be extended or they should move to another place. Serge found a hotel directly on the coast, in Park Lanzheron. They dragged their belongings to the car and went to search for this hotel with the romantic name 'Brigantina.' Certainly, he was glad to have an opportunity to stay in the place where they once met. It was their dear Lanzheron.

***

The story of the meeting of a young man and a girl, though, was only an instant in the history of Lanzheron, a park founded by Count Alexander Fedorovich Lanzheron. This legendary person participated in many fights, battling for Russia and its interests. In 1815, he was appointed as the town governor of Odessa, and managed to leave a kind memory of himself. His tenure brought about the first city newspaper (*Le Messager de la Rus Meridional*), the establishment of mineral water in the city park, and the layout of the botanical gardens which gave rise to gardening for all of Odessa. In 1817, he opened the Richelieu Lyceum, the second in Russia after Tsarskoselski. His house, with the famous cannons at the entrance, gave its name to Lanzheronovskaia Street, and served for a long time as one of Odessa's brightest sights. Up to now, the towering Triumphal Arch leading to the dacha of the Count, called by Odessans the Arch of Lanzheron, opens on the road to a beach of the same name.

Lanzheron Park was extolled by many Russian poets and writers, such as Iuri Olesha, Vladimir Glazyrin, Konstantin Paustovsky, and Valentine Kataev.

First, the dryness and wildness of the neglected park
Then the road down, and a stone arch,
Absolutely Italy.
A curvy, olive trunk
Hanging in emptiness,
Glowing in brightness,
And the sea flat, like a table.
I knew, I felt, that later or early
I will return to my homeland …

This is how at a mature age, Kataev described it.

***

In short, the Arch Lanzheron, the park descending to the sea, and the beach itself—are all symbols of Odessa.

An inexplicable nervousness filled Serge when he taxied up to the Triumphal Arch. From here he started to watch the girl in far away 1973. But today, she sat near him on the front seat of the car, and he was touching her when he shifted the lever of the transmission gears. He could stretch out his arm and embrace her, and he really did embrace her when the car stopped to park right near the arch … He was very excited and did not get out of the car for a long time.

He learned that cars were not permitted in the park: you could walk by foot or wait for the special tourist bus which carried interested persons to the hotels standing near the sea. Dragging the suitcases was inconvenient, so they decided to wait ...

Going down in the minibus took about five minutes. The hotel was private, and it immediately expressed its character of service. The suitcases were delivered to the room. Serge and Janna were offered a supper and soft drinks, but they refused everything and decided to walk in the park. First, they walked the asphalt path alongside the sea. Waves crawled softly over the coast and made the sand rustle. The seagulls soared in the air, and shouted something to each other—then easily sat down on the water. They had their own business. They didn't need to rent a room in the hotel. Their house was the sky and water. However, somewhere on the coast they built their nests. There they hatched nestlings and again headed to the sea.

The water was light green. Who decided to name it the Black Sea—is not clear. He truly, was a color-blind person. Then again, in the Red Sea the water is not red either. And the White Sea—not white. To hell with it, thought Serge, becoming tired of reflecting on the geographical oddities. A velvet September evening shrouded their walk. They went upwards along an alley, arguing about what falls from trees—buckeyes or nuts. Both were great experts in botany. So it was necessary to ask a man, who stood at a booth and selling some knickknacks.

"It is a nut," he said seriously. But he immediately understood that he would not receive any benefit from this.

"But this clip is for your wonderful ears!" He handed Janna some cheap costume jewelry: it looked like two cockleshells smeared by a varnish.

"How much?" Janna asked, simply to keep up the conversation.

"Only twenty-five grivnas.[54]

"And in dollars?" The American understood only one currency.

"Five dollars," another dealer shouted next to them.

"And what, we wouldn't understand without the help of a snot-nosed kid, or what?" cut off the first dealer, looking with disdain at his colleague.

"And how will you count the dollars without this old Jew?" said the man, referring to himself.

"Yes, we will figure it out, 'arithmetician.' Do you like to count someone else's money, huh?"

"But did you ever see a Jew who did not count another's money? Do you need it in shekels, young lady?"

"No, that's fine," Janna answered with a laugh.

"Well then, try some dried smelts and shrimp. What is the point of wandering without business?"

Janna, with a smile, turned and went down the hill. And Serge bought shrimp, most likely as a tribute of gratitude for the gratis performance. But when he crunched the shells,—1973 grew before him, like a rock from a fog. Then they also walked along the quay. He chewed the shrimp and spit out the chitinous tails. She went behind him, or beside him, or in front of him ... And here, everything repeats ... The magical cocktail of sadness and delight poured through his body. He can stretch out his hand and touch her. He can embrace her. He can kiss; everything is like in 1973. She turned: "I saw you back then, when you walked behind me!"

"You could not see me. You did not turn around."

"I turned around. You did not notice."

"I could not *not* notice. I looked at you all the time."

---

54 Grivnas—Ukranian currency.

"Let's check this out: I will go ahead, you don't take your eyes off of me, and I bet, you will not notice when I look at you."

The experiment started. Serge intently stared at Janna's nape. Yes, the head turned, but not so that he could get into her field of vision.

"So what, did you see?"

"I saw nothing."

"But I noticed you."

"That's impossible! What are you, David Copperfield in a skirt?"

"What skirt? I'm wearing red pants!" (She had on training pants, red in color.) "You are so observant. Back then, you only looked at my butt."

"Why bother looking at your covered butt? But it looked to me like your legs were sticking out from your ears. Now *this* phenomenon interested me ..."

"Ah, a Young Naturalist![55] ... I need to extend my legs." She put both hands on the elastic band of her red exercise pants, and with a jump lifted them upward. Her legs really did become longer.

"Ha-ha-ha, how did you like that method?"

"You need to change your profession—you will become a millionaire. Ladies and gentlemen, step right up!

Now on center stage, the unique Janna, stretching her legs up to her ears. A performance unmatched anywhere in our city! Only two soldo!"[56]

"Assisted by ... uh ... uh, just a passer-by, who happens to have the same last name ..."

Serge approached, and grabbed her training pants.

"Where should I pull: up or down?"

---

55 The Young Naturalists were a club of children in Russia who were interested in nature.
56 Soldo—old gold coin from ancient Italy.

"It's too early for down: up, for now."

But Serge could not contain himself, and embraced her and kissed her cheek that seemed to be burning with fire ...

***

"I can make you a chicken chop, and add tomatoes, cucumbers, potatoes, and certainly, greens. What kind of sauce do you want? What kind of drink would you prefer?"

The waiter, who was also the cook and the assistant to the owner of the hotel, was a young guy with an open kind face, and seemed born to be the master of service. He did not forget to bring a small pillow for their seats, and afghans to warm them. He lit a candle on the table. After all these preparations, the little table became very cozy and romantic. Nearby, in view of the lights from the hotel, the now-black sea stirred. Somewhere in the distance, with flickering lights, a big ship floated. On the table, an uncorked bottle of wine materialized, and glasses. Andre—this was the name of the waiter—poured the wine into the glasses, and placed napkins and silverware on the table.

"My God, this is some kind of paradise," Janna contentedly sighed. "Odessa, Lanzheron, wine, you beside me. Why didn't we find a hotel like this earlier?"

"I repent." Serge confessed. "But you must remember the time we arrived in Odessa. Almost at night. We didn't have too many choices."

"Ah, yes. Well, that was good too. I liked the deep leather armchairs in the restaurant."

"And cuisine was quite good," he pointed out.

"But here is an absolute fairy tale ... When do we leave?"

"It would be good tomorrow."

"Let's stay for one more day."

Serge looked pensive. His business in Moscow did not give him much time off. But he did not think for long, and nodded his head in assent. He became somewhat more relaxed and joyful from this decision. He drained his glass. Andre appeared like clockwork, holding in one hand two large fragrant dishes. During supper, there were no more trips into history. They actually talked about nothing; just light and nonchalant chatting. Serge thought about dumping the afghan, undressing, and diving into the dark, already cold autumn sea. But he remembered that the days of his youth had already passed, and instead he buried himself tighter in the afghan. He looked at Janna and felt very happy. He avoided thoughts of parting. Why think about the bad when it is possible to think about good?

"Oh, I ate too much." Janna spoke with a full happy voice. "I wanted to lose weight. It is like two hells, trying to lose weight, here with you!"

"Are you done? You know I love you the way you are. Relax ..."

"And the kilograms?"

"Which ones?"

"Extra."

"Where are they? I don't see them. Hey, kilograms!?" Serge glanced under the table. "There are no kilograms there."

There were, though, her legs tightly covered by the training pants, and her soft white sneakers. Serge straightened up, furtively looked at Janna, and felt that a *force majeure* attracted him to her. Why? He could not explain it to himself. He could not put it into words why it was so good now, even if he tried. It seemed to him that the long years of ridiculous separation had ended, and it would always be like this. There would always be the whisper of the sea, there would be a cool evening in a golden autumn, there would be an obliging waiter, and there would be a tasty meal. But the main thing, there would always be a room with his beloved from whom he never wanted to part, not ever ...

***

... The hotel balcony overlooked the bend of the Dniester River. Morning. The sun had crept out of its shelter. The banks of the river were densely overgrown by thickets of deciduous trees. They were decorated in green, yellow, red and claret. Above the quiet, almost immovable water rose a light fog. Silent and peaceful. There is no desire to move. You want to be suspended in the dense cool air, to be dissolved in it and to hang above the river. But you have to leave. Who needs it? Why is it needed? Why do you need to leave the place where you feel so good? ... Serge looked at the smooth gray-green surface of the water by himself, and somehow fell into his memories.

"Many years ago my Odessan uncle—actually, not even an uncle, but a distant relative, more like a kissing cousin—took me, a teenager, to the Dnestr River to fish. We rode for a long time by bus over a potholed country road. Then we walked for a long time to the village which was sheltered on the coast. My uncle puttered for a while with the boat motor, and then we floated for a long time upstream, disappearing in narrow channels, leaving the smooth surface of the flat river. At last, we reached the deserted coast where we set up our tent. We stayed for a week. Waited for the fish. But someone, higher up the river, opened the spillway of a dam. The water arrived and washed out the fish's food source, so they left. The fish were not interested in our bait. And those, that did nibble, simply went crazy. We caught half a small bucket of these mad fish. To come back home with such a poor catch was simply indecent. My uncle and I went to the fish farm and bought two full strings of carp. At home, my grandmother salted the fish: she simply poured large salt crystals on the fish and hung them on a cord at the window. In two days the fish became rotten. Fat worms crept over them. They felt good from grandmother's care. But soon, they went straight to the garbage pail. So my sortie to Dnestr ended. And here I am again. Strange. More than forty years have passed."

The Hotel Tiraspol is in the Prednister territory—not a recognized republic. Who will recognize it, and when, is not clear. There was an uprising in the beginning of the nineties, when human passions boiled over. People for some reason beat each other, and even killed. And for what? In the Prednister River region there was the 14th Russian army. And, General Lebed was restoring order. Now a small population lives here who sees rescue in its independence. They do not want to depend neither on Moldova, nor on the Ukraine. But their land sits directly between the two. The people living here thought up money that looks like candy wrappers from chocolates. They built their statehood, and opened their own cheap cafes. They even have a hotel with luxury rooms where they dragged in Jacuzzis, which made the room "heavier" up to fifty dollars a night. But Serge and Janna were not attracted by such comfort, and they hid away in their two-room suite. But, there was not enough furniture for two rooms. In one was a double bed. In another—for some reason, a single armchair. Probably, so one could sit and behold the naked walls.

They crossed the border of this small republic, late at night. And, in spite of the fact that they planned to leave it the next morning, the border guards sternly ordered them to register. The whole registration consisted of a stamp on an immigration card, but something awful and ridiculous is contained in this most 'Important of State Services' that was located God knows where, and all they could do was wander in the dark city and ask casual passersby for the address of the services.

Certainly, there was no opportunity to watch for traffic signs. Serge valiantly turned on a street with one-way traffic, and quickly rolled against the oncoming traffic. However, it was difficult to call it oncoming traffic, just, two or three cars passed by. And suddenly the joyful spark of a black and white striped police baton insisted in the darkness that it was necessary to stop ... "They got me," thought Serge.

"Comrades," said the face, "you committed a violation." (The word 'comrades,' not pronounced in Russia since the beginning of Perestroika, caressed the ear. Here, still, was the Soviet Union. Well, simply *The Lost World!*)

"Here it is expected ..." droned the rejoicing keeper of order, secretly counting the profits that would pour from the wallets of these two dolts.

"Open the window, quickly," said Janna resolutely, pulling out from her purse her American navy-skinned passport as if it was the ID of Queen Victoria.

The speech that followed poured out with such speed that to reproduce it is possible only by strongly straining the memory: "Listen, guys! It is so good that we found you!" (Duh, like we were looking for them!) "I am a correspondent for the American newspaper *Columbus*

Pictures. I am collecting material about border guards, and guards of order in your young surprising republic. In short, about those who are looking after the tranquility of this country. Help us, please ..." Janna had already run out from the car and came close to the thin youth, who had probably received his police uniform only yesterday. He even recoiled. Certainly, he in no way expected that, out of the dusty car with Moscow tags, the representative of a terrifying American publishing house would creep into the bright light. "How are you doing here with the crime sprees?" Janna pressed.

"Oh, it's OK, it is quiet ..." mumbled the sergeant.

"Can I have your ID? And your surname, your first name, is it possible to learn your ID number?" He answers, but Janna does not hear and does not write it down. "I will definitely write about you!" she promises solemnly.

The second, the little bit older one, asks Serge, "What, what newspaper?" Serge shifts his glasses on his nose and with a strong American accent, which he never had since the day he was born, said, "Buffalo Rangers."

"Yes, guys," shares Janna. "We urgently need to get to the hotel, and still have to register. Where all this is, we have no idea. And tomorrow, we have a meeting with the local press. We need to gather texture—in a word; we have business up to our necks." Serge imagines, how tomorrow morning, lying in bed, they would gather full bags of texture—it would be good to know, what kind of rubbish this is ...

In the meantime, the peacefully tuned guards of order have hospitably agreed to help, and asked them to follow their car. The jalopy with blinking lights, which was most likely a trophy from the time of World War II, gave them confidence, and the cortège quickly reached the place where the sacrament of registration was performed. The small window was covered by iron rods, coming out directly on the street. In it was an almost young woman with tousled dirty hair and a stupid— til you get a heart burn[57]—physiognomy. It was the dead of night. The brain, already-asleep, seemed incapable to resolve the problem of two pieces of paper, on which the same last names were written in two different alphabets. "What the hell is this? These are our guests from America, don't linger," insistently recommended the oldest one. Serge wanted to add, that they have to gather a lot of texture ... but knew he couldn't possibly suppress the neighing of a young stallion.

Her sight passed from one passport to the other, then back to the first ... The lady disappears somewhere in the depths of the passport sanctuary: her butt expressing complete bewilderment. At last she returns and demands money for her activities. Such money is simply not present, and there is no place to exchange the currency. Then the compassionate policeman pays her off himself. Janna says that the article would still go into the *Washington Post*. The policeman stands up even straighter and adjusts his uniform ...

Again, with their honorable escort, the car moved along the sleeping city. "Here is the hotel." A naked government building. The woman-manager simply melts from such visitors and wishes to thrust the newly made journalist and her companion into a Jacuzzi post haste. But the visitors eventually negotiated for a different empty room. Serge offered the policeman a few dollars. But that one refuses with pride. He salutes and disappears.

"Do you want to know what 'texture' is?" asks Serge.

"Na-uh, but what is it?"

---

57 An expression indicating until your are sick in your stomach.

"I think, it is the pattern of a tree when it's cut down ..."

Janna fell down on all fours, writhing in laughter.

***

The Dnestr smoothly moves its waters. It couldn't care less what is happening on the banks. It didn't care less one hundred, or two hundred years ago. It won't care less for a thousand more. What is its business with two people who are standing on the balcony and finishing their morning coffee? In a few minutes these people will go downstairs, sit down in different cars, and go: one to the West, and one to the East. The desire to scream is unbearable: there is no more time for partings and travels in different directions! But circumstances are beyond their power. They cannot control them so far. Therefore the suitcases snapped shut, announcing that this wonderful summit, after so many years, is over.

The taxi driver patiently waits for farewell kisses to run dry. The lips do not want to leave each other. The lips want to live together. They do not want to live anymore in loneliness ... when will they be next to one another again?

Serge with effort, extricates himself. He sits down in the car and presses on the gas. He drives away from the glorious and becoming dear Tiraspol. Ahead—a cloth of flat road. It is about 40 kilometers to the border. Almost nobody is on the road. And here, a hard lump catches in his throat. He lights a cigarette, but it does not help. Betraying tears flood his eyes. In 1974, in that ill-fated court, he should have just stretched out his hand and said: let's get the hell out of this office ... But he did not do it, and now bellows, threatening to go astray and roll into a ditch. It would be better to die. But not now, not now. "Unless your love for this woman has disappeared?" he asked himself. "But until it disappears—I need to live. In fact it will not disappear, so only death will interrupt it. But not now, not now ..."

***

The coals burn down. Serge's eyelids are closing. He sighs. It is a farewell sigh. He will not remember the past any more. And she won't either. So they agreed.

A future is waiting for them, a joint future ...

Author's Note

Thank you for reading *Love Is Never Past Tense*…

If you enjoyed it, please let me know. You can …

Write me: janna@loveisneverpasttense.com

Like the Facebook Page:
https://www.facebook.com/loveisneverpasttense

Follow us on Twitter:
@NeverPastTense

Check the web page:
http://www.loveisneverpasttense.com/

See and like the *Love Is Never Past Tense* book trailer on
http://www.youtube.com

If you enjoyed this book, I invite you to please write a customer review of the book at the retailer of your choice.

Janna Yeshanova
October, 2013

Janna Yeshanova, M.A., M.Ed., founder and principal of Life-Spark LLC, is a dynamic and powerful life coach, premier trainer and motivational speaker. Janna leverages her passion and engaging style to help others to overcome adversity and spark the possibilities of their lives. *Love Is Never Past Tense* ... was published first in Russia and Ukraine in 2009. It's a fascinating adventurous romance fiction, based on a true story.